I0451560

COWBOYS MINE

EVERNIGHT PUBLISHING ®

www.evernightpublishing.com

Copyright© 2020

Stacey Espino

Editor: JS Cook

Cover Art: Sour Cherry Designs

ISBN: 978-1-77130-814-4

ALL RIGHTS RESERVED

WARNING: The unauthorized reproduction or distribution of this copyrighted work is illegal. No part of this book may be used or reproduced electronically or in print without written permission, except in the case of brief quotations embodied in reviews.

This is a work of fiction. All names, characters, and places are fictitious. Any resemblance to actual events, locales, organizations, or persons, living or dead, is entirely coincidental.

COWBOYS MINE

Out of suffering have emerged the strongest souls; the most massive characters are seared with scars.

—Kahlil Gibran

COWBOYS MINE

COWBOYS MINE

Stacey Espino

Copyright © 2014

Prologue

12 years earlier

Eva glanced at the clock on her night side table with heavy eyes. It was well past midnight, the gentle cast of moonlight giving her bedroom a wash of grey. A strip of light from under the door caught her attention—and then the yelling from downstairs.

She crept from her room, wincing when the hinges on her door whined. There were two voices—one was her father, the other Colton McReed from the next ranch over. What was he doing at their house at this ungodly hour? She pressed her body against the wooden rails of the stairwell, where she could get a glimpse of the kitchen below. Darkness shrouded her on the second level, the cool hardwood chilling her bare thigh.

"What do you have to say for yourself, Colton?" Her father's voice was controlled but she recognized the serious edge to his tone. It was the same voice he used when he caught her lying or skipping out on her chores.

"What?"

"You broke the windows in my tool shed, and you're going to pay for them."

Eva gasped when she heard the accusation. Colton was fourteen, four years older than her. She worried that her father might give him a whooping.

"Well, I ain't! What are you gonna do about it? Hit me?"

"You're drunk. Come morning you'll work off your debt on my land," her father said matter-of-factly.

"I don't care about any debt. And I sure as hell don't care about you or your land!" Colton was belligerent and loud enough to wake the dead. She hoped her mother didn't catch her spying on something Eva knew was none of her business. When she caught movement at the edge of the kitchen, she realized Colton had shoved her father. She gasped aloud and then slapped her hand over her mouth. Her heart raced as she tried to get a better look.

"I know about your daddy, son. Everything will be okay."

This comment appeared to enrage Colt. She heard the wooden chairs topple over, and then violent shoving and harsh grunting ensued. "You don't know anything!"

Her father had to tackle him and hold him down on the floor, but he continued to try and throw punches. Colton may still be a kid but he was as big as her father at fourteen. From where his face was pressed to the laminate, she swore he looked straight up at her, even though she knew she was concealed in the dark shadows.

"It ain't your fault." She wasn't sure what was happening, but her father's voice held a note of sympathetic understanding despite the circumstance.

"I hate you! I hate you!"

"Everything will be okay," her father repeated, holding down his thrashing body.

Colton struggled like a mad man, throwing out curses that rang her ears, but her father held him still. Then, seemingly out of nowhere, he lost his steam and began to cry.

She'd never seen a man cry before, not her father, Colton, or his twin brother. It took her by surprise. Colton wept in deep, desperate waves, as if he'd lost his very soul. Her dad shifted his weight off Colt's back and pulled him into an embrace as they both sat on the kitchen floor. He held Colt's head to his chest and let him cry, not saying a word.

It wasn't until years later that she learned it was the night Jess McReed ran out on his family.

Chapter One

Present Day

Colton reached across the table for another tea biscuit. Eva's mother swatted his hand as he pulled back, but he only laughed before settling in his seat. His spurs chimed and leather chaps creaked as he adjusted his chair.

"You realize you have a home, Colton McReed," her mother said in mock irritation.

"Yes, ma'am, but you know how much I love your cooking."

"You can leave some for the rest of us for God's sake," North grumbled as he forked scrambled eggs into his mouth.

"Watch your mouth, young man." Her mother scolded him despite the fact he was twenty-six and twice her size. But Colton and North McReed were like part of the family. Eva barely noticed their presence because they were as natural in her life as her own reflection.

"Sorry, ma'am."

Everyone continued to eat in comfortable silence after her mother returned to the sink to tend the dishes. Her father was already out on the fields, tilling the land he'd harvested last week. All Eva could think about was the trip she'd be making in a few days. Her nerves were rattled considering the long drive and unexpected variables that could come up. She'd be entering her two cows in a competition at the annual rodeo in Chester. The prize was fifteen hundred dollars, and any extra money was welcome on a working farm. It was a chance to make her father proud and prove to him she wasn't a little girl anymore, but a capable twenty-two-year-old woman.

It was a two-hour drive to the rodeo, located in one of the larger cities to attract tourists. Eva had never been out of her hometown. All she knew was farming and her small circle of friends and family. Thinking of the trip both excited and terrified her.

"You tell the boys about your entries?" asked her mother without turning her back. The clang of pots and pans was the only sound left in the kitchen.

Eva gritted her teeth, wishing her mom hadn't mentioned the trip. Colt was frozen in place, his fork halfway to his mouth. North had already pushed his plate away and sat straighter, both hands braced on the edge of the table. The McReed brothers were like overbearing watchdogs, convinced it was their right to approve of every move she made.

"No, it never came up." She quickly gathered her dishes and cleaned her spot, eager to put as much distance between her and the house as possible. From her peripheral vision, she could see their attention was still fixated on her.

"What entry?" asked North.

She sighed dramatically. "Nothing. It's nothing." Then she grabbed her sweater off the coat tree by the side door and slipped out. The air had a note of coolness in it now that summer was nearly at an end. She had a million things to do—mucking out, cleaning the chicken coop, and putting up the storm windows in preparation for the fall season. First she had to feed the dogs.

"Hey, little miss. You didn't answer me." North's deep voice was followed by the smack of the screen door falling back into place. She kept walking.

Eva crouched low in the spare stall where they kept the dog food and began scooping it into the metal bowls. A moment later, North's large shadow blocked out the light from the bay doors.

"Go away, I'm busy." She knew he wouldn't leave her alone until he knew every detail of her trip. Part of her enjoyed tormenting the brothers. The Lord knows they'd done enough of it to her over the years. They'd dressed one of the pigs in her favorite dress for Halloween, filled her boots with manure, and trapped her in the hayloft without a ladder. Although they weren't annoying teens anymore, she still thought of them as oversized terrors.

"It's cute that you think I won't find out what you're up to." North leaned against the side of the stall, buttoning up his checkered jacket.

When she heard the sound of spurs echoing in the center of the barn, Eva knew she was outnumbered. She dropped the feed scoop into the bag and pushed past North. "Colt, tell North to leave me alone. I have too many things to get done without entertaining him."

Colton wrapped his arm around her waist and pulled her flush to his body, giving her a friendly kiss on the forehead. "We'll both leave you be after you fill us in on your entry. I know it wouldn't have anything to do with the rodeo in Chester, now would it?"

She rolled her eyes and let out the breath she held. "I'm entering Bessie and Ruby. The grand prize is fifteen hundred dollars."

Colton shook his head. She looked up into his blue eyes, but they were already narrowed and set. "How do you plan to get there? Your daddy taking you?"

Eva shifted out of his embrace. "I'm going alone. I'm a grown woman, not a child. And I think I'm quite capable of carting two cows in a trailer. I do it all the time."

"Not in the city, you don't," North corrected. "Don't you realize the trouble you could get into in a place like that?"

"I don't plan on getting into any trouble."

"The cowboys that flock to those places are not the type you're used to, Eva. Scam artists and predators are commonplace at the big rodeos. They'll eat you alive." Colton adjusted his Stetson as he countered her steps.

"Promise I'll be careful," she said dismissively. "Don't you two have a herd of cattle to bring in?"

She saw his jaw twitch but he didn't argue with her. Both men watched her until she returned to the stall to grab the bowls of kibble. By the time she stepped back out, they were gone. She sighed in relief, surprised they'd actually listened to her. Eva was another step closer to her new adventure.

****

"I ain't letting her go," said North. He knelt on one knee in front of the airtight fireplace, blowing at the embers.

"She's got her mind set."

"Don't care." North added some kindling to the growing flames. The evenings could get bitterly cold now. It was time to start building their wood stockpile out back. Their mother already had most of the tomatoes and apples jarred and stored in the cold cellar.

It was hard getting their own work done when they offered to help Mr. Ford with his cattle and other odd jobs, but he was more than a neighbor, and saying "no" was never an option.

"Tomorrow we'll talk with Ford. We'll make him see the danger of letting her go to Chester alone," said Colton. His brother lounged on the sofa, watching the leaves blow across the front of the picture window. The sun was half set, the sky matching the fall scenery—a mix of oranges and reds. They had no television, and they were both too tired to hit the bar most nights.

"That's right. By the time I'm finished filling him in, he won't let her pass town limits."

Colton shrugged one shoulder in nonchalance. "She'll kill us for interfering."

"Better than the alternative," he assured. After carefully inserting two good sized logs into the fireplace, he closed and secured the iron door and rose to his feet. "It's for her own damn good."

"She's twenty-two now, North. How long you gonna baby her?"

He scowled at his twin. "So, you're okay with her heading to Chester alone? God knows what trouble she could get into. An innocent farm girl around all those seasoned sharks?" North chuckled without humor. "Fuck that."

North headed down the hall toward his room, hesitantly stopping at the first door. He rested his hand on the knob for several moments before turning. Some days he didn't want to care, wanted to be so numb he didn't give a fuck about anything—but those were just passing temptations. He took a cleansing breath and then slowly opened the door. The light from the hallway filtered in so he could see the body-shaped lump under the blankets. Once he saw the gentle rise and fall, he let the door gently click shut again.

It was bad enough half the town looked down at them, referring to them as trash or bastards, but the whispers about their mother made it intolerable. He blamed everything on their father, the violent drunk who did them the favor of abandoning them without a dollar or a memory worth keeping. The only family they had nearby was their Aunt Laura. She knew about their mother's condition and continually offered to get her help. But their mother wasn't ready to accept she had a problem.

He continued on to the last room, kicking the door shut once he entered. Anger welled up inside him. More than that. He was frustrated and torn. He rammed his fist into his closet door, savoring the sting on his knuckles as he broke through the paneling. North unbuckled his belt and unbuttoned his flannel shirt. He stood in front of his dresser, staring at himself in the mirror for a long while—hating what he saw. While Colt had dirty-blond hair and blue eyes like their mother, North's hair was as dark as his eyes. If they weren't twins, nobody would believe they were brothers. He didn't give two shits about his appearance. He just hated the fact that the image reflecting back haunted him, a constant reminder of a man he'd rather forget. The man who'd taken everything from them.

North tossed his shirt so it landed on the edge of the mirror, blocking the unwanted image from view. He dropped down on the bed, the mattress protesting until it finally settled. There was something about autumn that made him feel more lost than he normally did. Everything was grey and dying, and more time was spent indoors rather than keeping busy with his hands.

He stirred for a while before finally giving up and bolting back to his feet. North paced his room, his mind drifting to everything unsavory. It would be so easy to forget his troubles with the help of cheap whiskey or the adrenaline that came from a good bar fight. Too easy. In the end, he slipped a padded jacket on over his bare skin and left the house. The wind and shadows swirled around him as he walked to the barn. He didn't bother with a saddle at his hour, just bridled and mounted his gelding before galloping off to the white brick house across the soy fields. Eva was a beacon of light in his dark, empty world. He may claim to be the one looking out for the

Ford girl, but in truth, he'd be broken without her.

He eased the horse to a walk when he neared the house. A warm glow emanated from the windows, and he imagined Mr. and Mrs. Ford sitting by the fire with mugs of hot cocoa. The grandfather clock would be ticking rhythmically, the small Shih Tzu curled up on the carpet, and there would be a sense of love and security that was nearly palpable. He felt like a nobody, an outsider looking in from the darkness, but rather than retreating, he prodded his horse to the rear of the house and dismounted.

North had planned to toss a small pebble at Eva's second story window, but his plan was foiled when he nearly crashed into Colt. "What the hell are you doing here?" his brother asked.

"Me? Last I saw you were falling asleep on the sofa. How'd you get here before me?"

They grumbled their joint displeasure, both looking up at Eva's window. "Well?"

"Well what? You gonna let her know we're here?" North tugged his jacket tighter to keep out the chill.

"She could still be pissed. You ready for a tongue-lashing?"

"You're afraid of Eva now? She's a hundred and ten pounds soaking wet."

Colt shoved him and started to climb up the metal antenna until in front of Eva's window. He rapped softly on the glass until she slid it up. "What are *you* doing here? And *you*?" She pointed accusingly down at North.

"Come on, it's cold, let us in," Colt pleaded.

"Why should I?" She crossed her arms over her chest. "You both take me for a child."

"Forget today, darlin'." Colt slid into her room head first, his boots shifting high as he toppled over the windowsill like an oversized sack of potatoes.

North climbed the same antenna and joined them. It was warm in her bedroom, a welcome contrast to the frigid night air. Eva's room always felt so small and delicate, like standing in a doll's house. The walls were painted pink and she had several shelves of teddy bears and trinkets, all staring back at him. If he moved the wrong way, it would spell disaster. He heard the muted laughter from Eva's parents' downstairs.

Colt crashed unceremoniously onto Eva's bed, the lush bedding enveloping him. He chuckled and rolled to his back, hugging one of her floral pillows. The only time he saw his brother happy was when they visited the Fords. Home was another story.

"Will you stop messing my bed, Colt. You're too big for your own good." Eva struggled to shove his legs aside so she could sit. But Colt reached up and tugged Eva down alongside him, her back pressed to his chest. He wrapped his arm around her, whispering something in her ear until she giggled.

North strolled around the room, examining Eva's prized possessions he'd seen a thousand times—the little pink elephant and her baby shoes mounted on an ivory plaque. Everything was so familiar, so comfortable.

"What's wrong with you, North? Come here."

He shrugged off his jacket, forgetting he had nothing on underneath. "Shuffle over," he said. When they'd made room for him, he settled in beside Eva, staring up at the ceiling and the small tin stars dangling down.

"You're sad again. Why?" she asked, her arm draping around his chest.

He shrugged.

Colt lifted his head. "She say something to you?"

"No, she's passed out good."

"You checked she was okay?"

"I checked, dammit!" His body tensed. "Can we not talk about her?"

Eva kissed his shoulder, holding him tighter. He closed his eyes and absorbed her goodness. "Is your mom sick?" she asked.

He swallowed hard, not able to answer. Colt spoke for him. "She'll be fine in a few days. She's just under the weather."

"Is there something I can do to help? Mom could bring her some soup."

"No, sweetheart. Don't you worry about her," said Colt.

They rested in silence, Colt occasionally brushing her hair with his fingers. It was so silky and long, the color of wheat. The scent of her strawberry shampoo drifted in the air, so feminine compared to the stench of cattle and horses North was used to.

She began to play with North's fingers, examining the various healing scars. When she beckoned for his other hand, she sat up in a rush. "What happened to you?"

"I'm not hurt," said North.

She kissed his torn knuckles, not repulsed by the bloody mess. "I'm telling mom. She'll fix you up good."

He took his hand back, not in the mood for coddling. "Later. Promise."

"You're stubborn as a bull."

North didn't respond. He just needed to be there in the fluffy pink blankets where he felt safe and loved. Eva could throttle him all she wanted.

She twisted around on her knees between them until she could see them both. "Dad says we're having a corn roast when I get back," she said with sudden enthusiasm, breaking the hush. "Even more people are coming than last year. It'll be fun."

"Did you invite the Blackwood sisters?" asked Colt.

Eva jabbed him in the stomach, making him grunt. "You can chase tail on your own time. Anyway, you'll be busy shucking. Lots of shucking."

Colt chuckled, tickling her until she squealed. North couldn't help but join in. It was so easy to tease Eva. They were both relentless, crowding her and offering no reprieve. He swore the bed would shatter into splinters with the weight of the three of them bouncing around.

"Stop!" she cried, half laughing. "Please!"

North stilled Colt's hand. He supported his weight over her body as she attempted to catch her breath. She looked up at him with her big blue eyes. Somehow Eva made life tolerable.

He desperately wanted to tell her everything.

But he refused to bring any of his darkness into her world.

Chapter Two

Eva brushed her oldest prized cow in long strokes. She'd raised Bessie and Ruby herself, keeping them separate from the herd. Her father rarely refused her, not that she ever asked for anything extravagant. She hoped at least one of them would win a ribbon or cash prize at the rodeo. Although her parents had babied her, she was twenty-two and felt the need to spread her wings. Most of the girls she'd grown up with here married, in serious relationships, or had traveled to the city to study in colleges and universities. She felt left behind, counting the days until she was considered an old spinster.

Her parents insisted she never had to worry about money, being an only child, because the family ranch would pass on to her. But how could she be expected to keep things running all on her own once her parents were too old to continue? Her dad already relied on help from the McReed brothers. What she needed was to fall in love, get married, and follow her own dreams.

Part of her felt the trip to Chester would be the catalyst to a new life. Although change was scary, it was often necessary to reinvent yourself.

"She's a beauty." Her father's gravelly voice sent a wave of calmness through her system. She smiled to herself as she continued to groom Bessie.

"Think she's a winner?"

"You have a fighting chance," said her father. "But I need to talk to you about the trip."

Now she whirled around. "Oh?"

"I was talking with Colton and North this morning. What they said makes sense—"

"You're cancelling the trip!"

"Hush now, darlin'. You're free to go to Chester with Bessie and Ruby—but you'll also be carting the McReed boys. They promised to look out for you while you're away."

She had to pause to take in what he'd said. When her father mentioned Colton and North, she was certain the trip was over. She'd kill them for opening their big mouths after their claim of a truce last night. But as much as she was pissed they'd be tagging along, at least she was still allowed to go.

"You've taught me how to use a rifle, daddy. I can take care of myself," she assured.

"I'd just feel better. You're my little girl, my only one, and I can't bear to have anything happen to you." He kissed her atop the head and then patted Bessie on the rump. "I'm sure you won't even notice the twins. They'll be busy having fun of their own."

True enough. Colton would be chasing after every new cowgirl he saw. She'd probably never see either of them. She returned to her task, her initial worry fizzling away.

Once she finished with Bessie, she moved on to Ruby. She was the smaller of the two, but she had a beautiful coat with unique markings.

"Hey there, pretty girl." Colton peeked from around the corner with a few wild daisies in his hand.

"I'm not talking to either of you. You promised not to make trouble, but you went running to my dad as soon as I turned my back."

He ran a hand through his shaggy blond hair and sat on the milking stool a few feet away. "We're doing this for your benefit, Eva. You think we have free time during fall harvest? We'll be up to our ears in work when we get home, plus we'll have to leave our mother alone for nearly a week."

"Then why bother?"

He was quiet for a moment, looking up at her as if she'd spoken a foreign language. "Because we love you."

She exhaled, all the bravado she'd built up since yesterday draining down to her cowgirl boots. As much as they drove her nuts most days, she loved the McReed brothers too, always had, always would.

"Well…thank you for offering. I'll help you with your chores when we get home."

He rose to his feet, setting the flowers on the stool before standing tall. And boy was he tall now. The brothers made her feel like a prairie mouse in comparison.

Eva tried to do everything around the ranch to ease the burden on her parents, but Colton and North were built like workhorses, able to do in an hour what would take her all day. She'd still try and help them when they got home, even if it was just doing laundry and cleaning chickens for their mother.

Colt ran a hand over Ruby's neck. "You'll win," he said with a smile. She was glad for the change of subject. She wasn't in the mood for fighting any longer.

Eva shrugged. "I have no idea what I'm up against. Guess I'm kind of nervous."

"Nervous? Look at Bessie. She's a regular butterball. I've been dreaming of turning her into steaks."

"Hey!"

He laughed, tugging her pigtail as he walked off. "Your dad's lending us the motorhome. I'll come after breakfast tomorrow and get it hooked up to my truck."

"See ya."

She planned to stop by their ranch after dinner and do what she could to help. She could clean, cook, bring in firewood, and do a million other things. Their mother shouldn't have to suffer because Eva was taking her sons away for a week. It was the least she could do.

****

North was ready to drop after pulling off his boots. He'd harvested more fields in one day than he'd ever done, hoping to get as much as possible finished before following Eva down to the city. The timing was shit, but he had no choice in the matter now. They'd made a promise to Mr. Ford and had to follow through.

Colton was in the shower, the static of water loud when he entered the quiet bungalow. He'd wanted to jump in himself, but he'd just wait until morning. His mother's door was open, and when he peered inside it was empty.

"Ma?"

There was no one else in the house, and he wondered where she was since her car was parked out front. He was tired of the lies, guessing games, and constant sneaking around.

North had saved extra for a rainy day, harvesting neighbors' fields during his free time. He'd left the money on the kitchen table in the morning so his mother wouldn't have to worry while they were gone. She'd be able to pick up any supplies, groceries, or gas she needed.

The money was gone.

He opened the fridge since she hadn't made anything for dinner. The white interior blinded him, only condiments and a drawer full of apples available. He closed it with a rattle and decided he was too tired to care. All he wanted to do was get to bed.

The front door opened, the cool breeze sneaking in. "Hey," said Colton, tossing his Stetson onto the hall table. He began tugging off his boots.

North frowned. "I thought you were in the

shower."

"Just finished bringing in the livestock."

Panic welled up inside him. He rushed over to the bathroom and pounded on the door. "Ma, you in there?"

When there was no response, he banged on the door more, the entire frame rattling. She had to be in the bathroom.

Colton joined him, bracing a hand against the wall beside the door. "Ma, open the door or we're breaking it down."

The shower was still going strong, humidity escaping from underneath the door. They looked to each other, a silent agreement passing between them. North reared back and rammed the door with his side and shoulder. It crashed open, the hinge snapping from the pressure. The shower curtain was half pulled off the bar and their mother was lying naked in the tub unconscious, the water streaming down on her body.

Colton grabbed a towel off the rack and dropped to his knees, covering her nudity and pulling her upper body up. North turned off the water.

"Ma, wake up! Talk to me," Colton shouted, lightly patting her cheeks.

North noticed the empty bottles of pills on the tiles, a few spilled out. His fears vanished and numbness took over. "She's fucking wasted." He kicked the bottles before knocking in the cupboard under the sink with his heel.

Colton carried her to her room, coming out a few minutes later. "She's okay. She's talking," he said.

"I ain't worried," he lied.

His brother exhaled. "She promised to stop. She's gonna take Aunt Laura's offer to get help in Newcaster."

North paced the room, throwing up his hands in defeat. "And you fucking believe her? She spent all the damn food money on pills again. What else is new? I'm sick and tired of her so-called promises."

"You'll get her upset if she hears you."

"What about me? Am I not allowed to get *upset*? Do you think it's normal to come home and find your mother high as a kite and nearly drowned in the bathtub, Colt?"

His peripheral vision caught movement to the right. Their mother was standing in the hallway, her pale blue bath robe wrapped around her. Rather than getting clean as promised, she'd reached a new low. North blamed himself. He never should have trusted her with cash money when her addiction was stronger than her resolve to quit.

"Fightin' over me?" Her words were slurred, a sign she was not even close to the sober woman he loved.

"You could have killed yourself," said North. "You know you can't keep doing this."

Her eyes widened when she was close enough to see him clearly. He knew what she saw, and it cut him deeper every time. "Don't *you* talk to me! I have nothin' to say to you, Jess. Get out of my house! Get out and never come back!" She staggered over to him, tears falling and arms flailing. He stood in place, not moving a muscle as she pummeled him with her closed fists. *"You bastard!"*

His throat clogged with emotion, his jaw set hard. This wasn't the first time it had happened, yet every attack hurt as much as the first.

"Ma, cut it out," said Colton, carefully restraining her arms. "It's just North, you know that."

"Get him out, Colton. I want him out of our house!"

Colton looked up at him with sympathy as he held her back. North turned around and made haste getting the fuck out of the house. He burst out onto the porch, savoring the burning cold against his heated flesh. Unshed tears were begging for release, but he refused to cry, refused to let himself be hurt by her again. Part of North wanted to hate her, to leave and never come back. The other part pitied his mother, knowing it was his no-good father that started her path of self-destruction.

He'd been glad his father left. At least it ended the years of harsh beatings. Their old man would use his fists or belt on them every time he'd come home drunk, which were most days, especially near the end. North took more than his share of abuse so he'd spare their mother. It was worth the added pain. When she began to mourn the fact her husband had left her, North felt a sense of betrayal, like all those years of suffering on her behalf were for nothing. Years later, she began to abuse different substances, finally settling on prescription drugs. Nearly every time she got high, she saw Jess McReed when she looked at North. It was one of the reasons he could barely stand to look at his own reflection.

He leaned over the porch rail, trying to settle his emotions while Colton got her tucked back into bed. She'd be fine in the morning, not able to remember a minute of tonight. But North would remember.

The steady beat of horse hooves approached. He looked out into the darkness, finding nothing until the golden Appaloosa appeared in the overhead lamp light. *Eva*. He stood up straight and met her in the front yard before she got too close to the house.

"Hey!"

"What are you doing here? It's late," he said.

"I came to help your mom. I would have come earlier but my dad gave me a list of chores longer than my arm." She smiled sweetly and attempted to dismount.

He pressed his palm against her thigh to keep her from getting off.

"You need to leave, Eva. Now's not a good time."

A blood-curdling shriek came from inside the house.

"What was that?" Eva prodded the horse forward until it was practically on the porch. She leapt down and raced to the door, swinging it open without hesitation. North was right behind her, grabbing her arm to keep her from entering.

Colton was struggling to settle their mother because she was in a fighting mood. He didn't want Eva to see their mother like this, or even to expose her to such a toxic environment. Eva represented everything good and wholesome in his life and he didn't want to spoil her.

"Oh my God, what's happening?" she asked, her hand over her mouth as she watched the train wreck of his life.

"It's him!" His mother pointed at the doorway where they stood. "Get that bastard off my property. He has no right to be in my house!"

"Get her out of here!" shouted Colton, his eyes pointed daggers when he saw Eva.

North pulled Eva out, but she tried to shrug him off, so he hoisted her up over his shoulder instead. "Put me down, North!"

He grabbed the reins of her mare and kept walking until they reached the edge of darkness. North set her down on her feet and passed her the leather lead. "Go home, Eva. I told you she was sick. This ain't no place for you tonight."

"Why was she saying those things to you? I don't understand."

"She's just sick," he repeated. Maybe if he said it

enough times he'd believe it himself. "I need you to listen and go home now."

Eva mounted her horse, and then she stared down at him. Her face was a mix of confusion and pity—something he didn't want from anyone, especially her. "Call me if you need me," she said just above a whisper. She turned the horse in the direction of the white brick house and then disappeared into the darkness.

Chapter Three

By seven o'clock in the morning, Colton was at the Ford ranch hooking up the mobile home. They'd always called it the silver bullet growing up. It was an older model camper with an upper sleeping area, small kitchen, and modest living space. It would be cramped with the three of them, but cheaper than the pricey hotels around the rodeo—if there was even availability, which he doubted.

The sky was clear so they'd have an easy trip along the highways and back roads. He hadn't spoken with his twin since last night, and the tension between them was thicker than molasses. He'd only gotten a couple hours sleep.

"I hooked the livestock trailer up to my truck already," said Eva. "Are you guys going to follow me with the camper?"

Colton hadn't even heard Eva approach, too lost in his own thoughts. He was thankful she didn't mention last night. It was much easier to live in beautiful ignorance. When he'd seen her in the doorway with their mother on a rampage, he felt a piece of his heart fracture. His two worlds were best kept separate. The Ford family was his saving grace, and he didn't want to burden them with their personal problems or embarrass their mother in front of neighbors when she wasn't herself. When sober, Karen McReed was a good country woman with a kind heart, everything he could want from a mother. He just wished those days were not so few and far between.

"One of us will be driving your truck. You can ride shotgun."

"I can drive my own truck, Colt. Don't start pushing me around already."

"If you want to be helpful, go check the back and see if the brake lights come on."

They tested all the lights and signals and Colton ensured the hitch was secure. Everything was ready to go once North showed up. He wasn't looking forward to seeing his brother. Last night had been brutal. The way their mother always lashed out at him when she was wasted, convinced he was their father, shredded North to pieces. But despite her verbal abuse and constant drug relapses, they still had hope she'd get better. Time was supposed to heal all wounds, but he was losing hope fast. Colton frequently told her there was more to life than Jess McReed, that she shouldn't be so affected by his actions and betrayal. But she seemed beyond repair, as if their father had taken everything noble and loving about her when he abandoned the family.

They leaned against the side of the camper, looking out into the fields. It was getting harder and harder to put on his happy face. The day was still early, only the occasional call from the rooster filling the air. Neither of them said a thing.

"Why didn't you tell me?" she finally asked, her voice hushed. Eva didn't turn to face him, her eyes still riveted on the landscape.

"There's nothing to tell."

"What about your mother?"

He frowned, fiddling with a piece of straw. "She's sick is all."

Eva shook her head. "That didn't look like any kind of sickness I've ever seen. If I didn't know any better, I'd say she looked ready to kill her own son."

He shifted to his side, forcing her to do the same. "It ain't your business, Eva Ford. Little girls shouldn't be horning in on other people's affairs anyhow."

Colton didn't need Eva raising a fuss in front of

North, upsetting him further. They had a long trip ahead of them, and he wanted his personal mess left behind.

"I'm not allowed to care?"

"No." He stepped away, massaging behind his neck with both hands. "Not about this."

"Does it have something to do with your father leaving?"

Every muscle in his body tensed, his blood running cold. Why did she ask him such a question after all these years? He thought it was common knowledge that it was a forbidden topic. Colton had no plans or desire to talk about the deadbeat who'd left permanent scars on his body and soul. As much as Colton swore he hated the vicious man before he left, it was immeasurably more painful when he'd walked away.

"Eva, don't," he warned. He may love the little Ford girl, but she was pushing the envelope. "Subject is closed. All you need to worry about is Bessie and Ruby. Understand?"

Eva could never fathom what he was going through. She was born and raised by the best family he'd ever known. All she knew was kindness, safety, and unconditional love. The biggest obstacle in her life was getting her prized cows to the rodeo. She lived in a counterfeit paradise, oblivious to the real-life issues just next door, never mind around the world. It was the reason they couldn't let her go to Chester alone.

Colton and North had been forced to man up as young men. They worked their land, supported their mother, and struggled to keep on the straight and narrow. Their mother was sliding down a slippery slope of addiction and refused to get help. Everything in their life was tainted in some unspeakable way. It was one of the reasons he was drawn to Eva. He felt that her light could somehow scare away a bit of the darkness surrounding him.

North rode up to the trailer on horseback, dismounting before stopping. "Everything's secure at home. You ready to go?" His chin was up, his shoulders back. All his brother's walls were firmly in place, a safety measure to avoid the pain. It was the same destructive cycle, and Colton wasn't sure how much longer his twin could hold onto his own sanity.

They'd taken the car keys and filled the fridge and cupboards with food before leaving. God willing their mother would keep her promise to keep clean while they were away. It was tiring playing the parent to his own mother. He'd called their Aunt Laura to tell her they'd be gone the week. She promised to come check on their mother, and he prayed she'd listen to her sister's advice to get clean.

"Trailers are hitched," Colt confirmed.

"I'll drive the trailer. You take Eva in her pickup."

He knew North would avoid Eva like the plague after what she'd witnessed last night. North liked to play house, to pretend life was peaches and cream to everyone looking in. By ignoring their grim reality, he was essentially living a lie, his only happiness found in a fantasy world.

"Fine." Colton found Eva around the corner and motioned for her to follow him. When they reached her truck, he beckoned for her keys.

"I can drive just fine, McReed."

He waggled his fingers, not planning to head out until he had them in his hand.

She crossed her arms under her chest, and he looked away. "Part of the reason I'm going to the Chester is to prove to my daddy that I can take care of myself. I'm not getting any younger, and the thought of growing old alone doesn't sit well with me. If he can't see me as a woman, he'll never let me grow up."

"You saying he doesn't approve of you taking a husband? You going to Chester to find yourself a man?"

Eva shook her head in exasperation. "Never mind. Let's go."

****

Eva ate some of the dried apples her mother had packed her. She watched the landscape change outside the passenger window, the farms getting smaller and towns larger. They'd already been driving for an hour.

"I've never been to the city," she said, hoping to make some friendly conversation. It had been too quiet in the cab of the truck, and she wasn't used to feeling uncomfortable around Colton.

"I know, Eva."

So much for that.

"You don't have to be mean."

"I'm just tired. I'll be happy when we get there, and ever happier when it's all over with."

She'd already decided not to mention what had happened the night before again, no matter how tempting. If the McReed brothers wanted the topic of their mother off limits, she had to respect that. It just seemed unnatural to ignore something so important. Eva had hoped they felt comfortable enough with her to tell her anything. She'd never judge them, never push them away.

Admittedly, she didn't know much about their history even though she'd known them her entire life. Their father had walked out on the family over a decade ago. She'd seen their mother many times, but she mostly liked her solitary existence. She even refused to join the prayer group, ladies' night, or the knitting club her mother belonged to, making excuses until no one bothered to invite her to anything. The brothers came to their house almost daily but never invited Eva over. Now she was beginning to understand why.

The McReed twins had a bad reputation around town. They were known as womanizers, brawlers, and drunks. Eva had a hard time believing a word of the gossip when they'd only been loving and patient with her. Her father trusted them unconditionally, despite the other cowboys in town warning him to keep them away from his only daughter.

"You didn't come in for breakfast today. You hungry?" she asked.

"I'm fine."

Eva punched Colton in the arm, garnering his full attention. He alternatively watched the road and her. "What was that for?"

"Stop being a jerk. We're going to be stuck together for a week, and I refuse to be at each other like cats and dogs. If it were up to me I would have come alone."

He shook his head. "That wasn't gonna happen. Besides, your father wouldn't have allowed it."

"After he talked with you," she reminded.

"The city is no place for a country girl."

Eva huffed, but she also felt the tension slipping away. Playful banter she could handle but having a rift between her and Colton or North was too much. Besides her parents, they were all she had.

"We'll see." She pulled up her legs and cuddled on her seat. The fields hurried by the window, an endless blur of greens and golds. She'd barely slept all night, replaying the terrifying events at the McReed home over and over in her head. The drone of the engine lulled her until her eyes were too heavy to keep open.

She was woken by the sound of a door closing.

After a brief bout of confusion, she sat up straight and looked out windows. There were people everywhere. She'd never seen so many people in one place in all her life. The rodeo was even busier than her father's corn roasts. Colton had parked the truck, leaving her alone in the cab. The area was laden with livestock trailers and pick-ups. She was glad the brothers were with her because she wouldn't have a clue where to start. Eva began to think Chester was out of her element.

She hopped out of the truck and looked around for North and the trailer. She saw it parked a few down the line. She adjusted her ponytail and took in her surroundings. There were horns, loudspeakers, music, and cattle clamoring. Vendors lined the streets selling everything from event tickets to hotdogs. The scent of popcorn and caramel filled the air. She was star struck, walking in a daze along the dirt path as she took in all the sights, sounds, and smells.

"Lost?"

She turned around and found a seasoned cowboy approaching from behind. He had chocolate brown hair and squinty green eyes. Her heart did a little flip when he tipped his Stetson in greeting.

"I'm new. I'm entering my cows in a competition." She continued forward, pointing to her trailer.

"Can I have a look?"

Eva smiled and unhooked the back door of the trailer, proud to show off Bessie and Ruby. "Let me know what you think," she said, waving him to enter the tight confines of the trailer with her.

He stepped up, his leather boots creaking, and he patted Bessie as he settled in beside her. "These are big girls. Very nice."

"I'd love to place…even if it's just a ribbon." She

turned slightly in his direction, taking the cowboy in from head to toe as discretely as possible. His cologne was rich and musky. His Wranglers were worn with age and low on his hips. "Are you riding?"

"Plum near every day." He shifted his stance and leaned against the side of the trailer, looking directly down at her. "You're the prettiest little thing I've seen in a long time. Just gorgeous."

She knew her face was heating and turning every shade of red. It wasn't often a man paid her a compliment. Around town, she was just one of the locals, invisible to the opposite sex. Men daring enough to pay her mind were usually scared off by Colton or North. She liked this new attention.

"My name's Wade, by the way. What's yours, sweet thing?" He took a section of hair from her long ponytail and felt it between two fingers. Eva froze.

She had to think for a minute before even remembering her name. "E–Eva," she stammered, suddenly suffering from the worst case of dry mouth.

"You should come and watch me ride. I'll be on tonight at six in the bull pit. I'd love to have you cheering me on. You'll be my good luck charm." He trailed the backs of his fingers along her jaw line. She leaned into his touch, nearly closing her eyes. Was she that starved for attention? It was only natural to feel desire for a man, she decided. She was no longer a girl, and women had needs.

The thunderous boom of the ramp dropping down into place made her jump. A very serious looking North stared at her when she looked back.

He hopped up into the trailer, coming into Wade's personal space. "Can I help you?"

"Eva was just showing me her prize cows." He turned in her direction with a wink. "Which I'm sure will take first place."

"You're sure of that now, are you?"

"North, cut it out." She shuffled out with Wade and promised to watch him at his event before he left. This could be the start of something big—true love, the passion of a lifetime.

When she returned to the trailer, Colton and North were both waiting for her. "Shouldn't we be unloading them?" she asked, hoping to avoid an uncomfortable conversation about the birds and bees. "I have to turn them in and get registered."

Colton ignored her, looking at the path Wade had just taken. "Who was that?"

"That was my new friend…Wade."

"Wade have a last name?"

She shrugged. "It doesn't matter. I'm sure I'll find out next time I see him."

"There won't be a next time, Eva." North crowded her against the side of the trailer, bracing his arm near her head. "You need to stay close to us and stop talking to strangers. You think *Wade* gives two shits about you or Bessie? All he cares about is what's between his legs."

"You're gross!" She tried to wriggle away, but he wouldn't have it.

North's voice softened. "I'm only looking out for you."

"He said I was gorgeous."

Colton chuckled. "He says that to anything with two legs and a pigtail, I promise you that."

Eva's mood soured. Wade had built her up so high in just a few minutes. She was soaring in the clouds. He was sincere and friendly, not looking to get into her pants. Not every man was a pig. But in a second she was brought down to Earth by the unforgiving McReed brothers and their seeds of doubt. Why couldn't they be happy for her? Just because they didn't see the value of taking wives for themselves, didn't mean she wanted to be alone forever, too.

"He likes me," she insisted. "Have you never heard of love at first sight?"

"You're in love now, are you, little one?" asked Colton, humor in his tone.

She shrugged.

"Horny cowboys are a dime a dozen at these rodeo events. Guarantee you he's already forgotten your name, darlin'."

"Thanks a lot, Colt. Just help me get the cows out."

Eva wasn't naïve enough to give her heart to the first stranger she came across, but she wasn't going to throw away any opportunities either. Wade was handsome and made her feel attractive and desirable. Just thinking of seeing him again at his bull riding event made her stomach flutter. She wondered if the McReed brothers would be a wrench in her plans the entire week.

After getting the animals checked into the holding paddock for new arrivals, they had to line up at the registration desk set up just outside a large barn. It was a mad house, people arguing and shoving, cursing, and threatening. Eva kept her mouth shut and stayed safely between Colton and North. There was a makeshift tarp set up to keep the direct sunlight off everyone waiting in line, but the rays still managed to get to where she was standing.

Another thing she noticed were the number of buckle bunnies hanging around the periphery, just waiting to sink their claws into an unsuspecting cowboy.

One of them wore a barely-there shirt, showing off her midriff. Her jean shorts didn't even cover her whole rear end. Eva knew the woman wasn't a real cowgirl because her boots didn't have a scuff on them and her make-up and hair were coiffed to perfection. It was all an illusion, a trap to snag her prey.

Eva didn't wear make-up. If she was lucky, she remembered to put on moisturizer in the morning. Her mother frequently told her about the benefits of keeping the skin supple and natural. When she noted Colton and North whispering and gawking at the scantily clad women, she looked down at herself and began to feel self-conscious. Her jeans were fitted but worn out, and her blouse covered all her skin except her forearms. But Wade seemed to think she looked good enough, and that's all that mattered. She hoped he didn't judge a woman by the size of their chest like the twins. They were so busy staring at all the cleavage that she had to prod them to move forward in the line every time it shortened.

After registering, they unhitched the trailer in the large field on the perimeter of the main event areas. Colton fell asleep within half an hour of entering the camper, and North rummaged through the small fridge. They'd had a long day and early start. Now it was almost dinner hour.

"I can't believe they made us come here today when the event doesn't start for five days," she said. "You could have had all that time to work your fields." She felt bad forcing the brothers to be idle when they had a massive workload back home. But they were the ones insisting on accompanying her.

"Everyone has to register today, Eva. If they don't, they're out," said North.

They sat on either side of the small, laminated table. North bit into an apple, the crunch obscenely loud in the small trailer. He wouldn't look her in the eyes, obviously still upset due to the drama from yesterday.

"You're still mad at me."

He scowled. "I'm not mad at you." After another bite of apple, he continued, "I just wish you hadn't come over without asking."

"Like you? You must crawl in through my window at least twice a week. Sometimes I don't even know you're in my room until I climb into bed."

"That's different."

"Really? How so?"

He leaned back in his chair, some of this stiffness softened. "You don't have any skeletons in your closet."

"I have plenty."

His interest piqued, an eyebrow lifting. "You turn red as a lobster when someone says the word *shit* in front of you."

"Do not!"

"You're a good girl, Eva. Don't try to deny it." He tossed his apple core on her side of the table.

"Jerk." And just like that they were back to normal. They could never stay mad at each other. North settled his head on his bend arm and fell asleep just before her eyes became too heavy to keep open.

Chapter Four

"Where's Eva?" North woke up to the wash of pink across the table. The sun was setting, darkness stealing the last bit of daylight. He'd checked the trailer, only to find Colton asleep in the upper bunk, his big feet dangling off the end.

"She ain't up here." Colton rolled over, uninterested.

"It's after eight. *Fuck!*"

He looked out the windows. Chinese lanterns were strung outside the makeshift trailer park. A bon fire blazed in the near distance, and a gunshot rang off. All the rodeo riders and drifters were getting ready for a night of debauchery. And little Eva was out there somewhere.

Colton climbed down, rubbing his eyes, his dirty-blond hair sticking up in every direction. "What time is it?"

"I already said it's after eight. Eva ain't here. God knows what trouble she's gotten herself into." North remembered the look of lust on that drifter's face earlier in the day. Even worse was the way Eva fell for his charms like a calf to the slaughter. All he could think about was knocking that cowboy into next week for looking at Eva with those wicked eyes.

"We'll take a walk. There are only so many places she could be at this hour."

After donning heavy plaid coats to keep out the evening chill, they headed out on foot to look for Eva. They came on the trip to protect Eva. They'd promised Mr. Ford that not a hair on her head would be out of place, and on the first night they'd lost her.

They weaved through the different campfires set

up throughout the campground, looking at all the blonde girls in hopes of spotting just one. Nothing. When they reached the epicenter of activity, the local bar, they decided to check it out. As soon as they opened the door of the country and western bar, the music and raucous laughter spilled out into the night.

"Let's split up," said Colt.

They went their separate ways, pushing through the rowdy cowboys in search of Eva. North felt like a bomb waiting to go off. Every time a man bumped against him, he clenched his fists in anticipation of a fight. All he kept imagining was Wade and his fucking silver buckle. A tap on his back stole his attention. When he spun around, ready for anything, it was Eva who looked up at him. The first thing he noticed was the top buttons of her blouse were left unbuttoned.

"What's going on?" he demanded. "Why in God's name are you in this shithole?"

"Wade bought me a drink." She held up a bottle of beer and giggled. He snatched it from her and set it on the nearest table.

"Unbelievable, Eva." North practically dragged her out of the bar. Colton must have spotted them because he was right behind them.

Once outside in the crisp, cool air, he cupped Eva's face and made her look him eye to eye. "What were you thinking?"

She shrugged away. "I watched Wade ride, and then he bought me a drink. I'm twenty-two, North. There's nothing wrong with going on a date."

"*A date?*" North couldn't believe what he was hearing. She'd known Wade all but a few hours, and now they were some sort of item? Eva was setting herself up for some serious heartache or much worse.

"I'm not twelve and I *don't* need saving." She

walked away from him, heading in the direction of the trailer. "Both of you need to give me some space."

Colton grabbed his arm before he could chase after her. "Relax. She's in one piece."

"But—"

His brother shook his head. North took a cleansing breath and began to follow behind Eva. Colt was right. If they pushed too hard, Eva would fight back harder. They had to play their cards right if they wanted to keep her out of trouble the entire week.

****

Eva was pissed off and thoroughly embarrassed. She didn't even have a chance to say good-bye to Wade since the McReed brothers practically dragged her out of the bar. The only reason she agreed to go along with them was to avoid any more humiliation. They were worse than her father, like overbearing mother bears.

She stormed into the trailer, letting the door slap back into place—hopefully right in North's face. She climbed up into the sleeping area, kicked off her boots, and disappeared under the covers. There was no way she wanted to argue all night. She just wanted to close her eyes and remember how good it felt being with Wade. He made her feel like a princess, buying her a drink and staying by her side most of the evening. She couldn't believe he wanted *her* when there were so many beautiful women in Chester. Eva was shy, inexperienced, and didn't own any fancy clothes. Wade was a champion rider with so much worldly experience. They could be a match made in heaven, but Colton and North were going to ruin everything.

"Stop being a sour puss." Colton crawled up the mattress beside to her. The flimsy bed sank due to his weight, forcing her body to roll in his direction.

"Go away."

He forced her to turn and face him, holding her wrist so she couldn't strike out. "Don't be running off after dark again, little miss, it's not safe."

"It wasn't after dark, and I was with Wade, not by myself."

"That's what I'm worried about."

Eva scowled, wishing she could get through to him, to make him understand it was her life to live. If she made mistakes, she'd learn from them. They couldn't coddle her forever. "There's nothing wrong with Wade. He's a perfect gentleman. He lives on a farm just south of here when he's not on the road."

Something dark crossed Colton's eyes. "I don't want to hear about him, Eva."

"Fine, let's just go to sleep then."

They were all exhausted, overly so. She only hoped things would be better in the light of day when they were all refreshed. And she needed to find out what events Wade was riding in tomorrow afternoon. She needed to apologize for her disappearing act and get to know more about him. He was reluctant to talk about his private life, so she was anxious to learn everything.

North joined them, flanking her other side. She felt like a sardine in a can with the two oversized cowboys stealing all the space—and the blankets. They started a silent tug-of-war until North finally agreed to share a blanket with her. He'd taken off his jeans and shirts. His bare skin felt hot, like cuddling up to a warm fireplace. She closed her eyes and leaned against him, breathing in his familiar scent. His presence put her at ease, her anger and worries fading away as she tried to fall asleep.

She was so busy hating Colton and North for cutting her date short that she forgot they were there for her benefit. They had their own lives to lead, and more problems at home than she could even comprehend. Eva still remembered the hurt in North's eyes, and she never wanted to see it again. Maybe the break from reality back home would do them all good.

The next morning, Eva awoke when the guys started tossing and turning in the small bed. She opened her eyes, glad to see the beams of sunshine coming in the windows. A new day was exactly what they all needed.

"I'm starving," said Colton, stretching out next to her.

North slipped down out of the bed. "Do we have anything to eat?"

"Mom stocked the fridge. We can make bacon and eggs," said Eva.

After washing up and partially dressing, they fought for space in the tiny kitchen. There was a hot plate and limited running water. Eva added the bacon to the frying pan while Colt scrambled the eggs in a mixing bowl beside her.

"What's the plan for today?" asked Colt.

"I have to tend to Bessie and Ruby this afternoon." Eva didn't mention her plans to hook up with Wade at some point. She decided her extracurricular activities were best kept from the meddling brothers.

"I heard they're paying a hundred dollars cash in a pig wrangling competition this morning," said North. He kept sneaking peeks at her, and she wondered if he knew what she was thinking.

"Knock yourself out," said Colton, setting the bowl aside. He poked his head over Eva's shoulder, using her as a shield from the bacon grease.

She tried to side-step, but he kept her in place. "Colt, everyone knows you don't fry bacon in the nude."

"Hey, I have my drawers on. Hurry up so I can cook the eggs." They only had one hot plate, so breakfast would take longer than it did at home—and wouldn't be nearly as good as her mother's.

North set some sliced bread on the table and poured three glasses of orange juice. "Mrs. Ford sure thought of everything," he said. "I still think we'll need more money. The food won't last all week."

They all sat down to breakfast once the eggs were scrambled. Colt and North reached across her plate like they did at home, not worrying about their manners. Eva was famished, not having eaten properly yesterday.

"If you want to roll in the mud with the pigs for cash, that's your prerogative," said Colt.

"You just know I'd kick your ass."

The brothers stared at each other between eating, some silent competition building up between them. They may be men, but they were really overgrown boys.

After dressing for the day, they all head out together. The crowds were already building around the different event paddocks. It was exciting, the energy snapping in the air. She'd always wanted to see a rodeo in Chester, but her father was never interested in anything to do with the city. He more than busy with his cattle operation at home to care about anything else.

They approached the sign-up desk for the pig wrangling, and she was surprised to see both brothers fight for the pen to sign up. She shook her head and went to find a good vantage point along the wooden slat fence surrounding the pen. It looked like half a dozen other cowboys had signed up along with North and Colton.

After nearly an hour of waiting, the announcer introduced himself and explained the rules of the game. She kept her eyes on the twins, ready to cheer them on. There wasn't a free spot along the fence. Eva leaned over, her heart racing when the starting gun went off. Although they didn't have pigs at home, she'd seen

North and Colton do well corralling loose chicken and cattle.

The mud began to fly almost immediately. Colt rushed over and handed her his Stetson, followed by North. "You're both on the clock," she shouted. The other men were already in the melee, diving into the slop in an attempt to grab one of the slippery pigs. When North stumbled in the mud, skidding along his stomach, she couldn't help but laugh out loud. Only his eyes were free from the sticky brown coating. Colt managed to grab a pig, but before he could carry it to the pen, it slithered out of his arms. The crowd was in an uproar, shouting and hollering the entire time. It was light-hearted fun, not serious business like the horse and bull riding.

The winner was the oldest cowboy, surprising everyone. The buzzer sounded and the competition was over for the day. As the crowd dispersed, the twins approached her spot at the fence. They were covered head to toe in brown mud—their exposed skin, hair, and clothing.

"You two are a sight. I wish ma could see you."

"We didn't win," said Colt like a sulking child.

She couldn't help but giggle.

He narrowed his eyes, reaching up under her shoulders to pull her into the ring with them.

"Don't you dare, Colton McReed!"

It was too late. Within seconds they both had their arms around her to ensure she was thoroughly coated in the same filthy mess. "Ain't a laughing matter now, is it, little lady?"

She scooped up an oversized handful of slop and tossed it at Colt. Within minutes the three of them were playing in the mud, trying to win some personal competition to stay the cleanest. They all failed miserably.

****

North fell on his ass too many times to count, his boots continually slipping in the pig slop. He hadn't won his hundred dollars as hoped, but it still felt good to let loose and have some good old-fashioned fun. Life back home was sobering. He needed this respite more than he realized.

Eva squealed when Colt smoothed more mud on her arms, tickling her sides when she fought back. North froze in place, suddenly mesmerized by the sound of her laughter. He watched her squirm and smile, her long blonde hair streaked with mud. His chest felt tight, something he noticed getting worse the past year.

"Save me," Eva pleaded as she wrestled with his brother.

He took a breath, pushed away his uncomfortable emotions, and rejoined Eva and Colton. She wrapped her arms around his neck after he pushed away his brother.

Eva looked up at him, the sun reflecting off her bright blue eyes. He'd never realized what a cute little nose she had. As he studied her closer, he was drawn to the swell of her lips.

"Had enough?" he asked.

"Maybe for one day."

He wanted to stay there forever, holding her close and staring into her eyes. Instead, he pulled away and ducked between the fence rails to get out to the pen. North was fucked up. He had no right to be looking at Eva with anything impure in his head. Maybe his mother was right about him.

They all looked like spectacles as they walked back up the main street. North dipped his hat to a few staring ladies passing on the far sidewalk. It was the only clean thing on him. They were all covered in quickly drying mud, and he didn't even have a red cent for his efforts. The trailer didn't have a proper shower, so they had to use one of the public buildings to get washed up. After gathering up fresh clothes, they headed to the public shower stalls.

"Go on, Eva. We'll stand guard," said Colton.

She looked in the stall skeptically, finally stepping inside with her shampoo bottle and tossed her towel and clean clothes over the doorframe. This was no place for a lady, especially Eva, and North had already made that clear before they even set out on the road in the first place. The rodeo was for hardcore cowboys and drifters. Spectators were smart enough to stay at local hotels or in fully equipped trailers, not relics from a bygone era like the silver bullet.

"No peeking," she called out once the shower started. It was a crude little structure like the other five lined up at the rear of the barn. Judging by Eva's unpleasant shrieks, there was no hot water, either.

"I ain't peeking. Hurry up in there so I can have my turn."

As he waited outside the stall with Colt, he scanned the area. There were countless gold diggers circling the events—bleached blondes with pumped up cleavage. He eyed a few with interest.

Eva was too damn good for him, and he dared not ruin the precious bond they shared. He just needed to get laid, to lose himself in the arms of a woman he could never lose his heart to.

Chapter Five

"She should have been back hours ago," said Colton. He sat at the kitchen table alternately watching the window and the clock. Seagulls descended on the field where a hotdog vendor had parked during the day. Everyone was packing up for the night.

Eva had checked in on Bessie and Ruby every afternoon for the past two days. She was never late coming home.

"Like you said, she's a big girl now," North said dismissively. "You sure you want to go dragging her home again?"

"You're usually the first in line. What's up with you lately?"

Colton couldn't help but scowl as he assessed his twin brother. They were too in sync for him not to notice a mood shift. This was a major one.

North propped both arms under his head as he lounged in the loft. "Nothing. I'm just starting to think that maybe Eva's right. Maybe we should be giving her more space."

"Are you playing with me?"

"*What?*"

Something had to be seriously wrong for North to suddenly stop caring about Eva. The little Ford girl was the only thing keeping either of them going some days. It was natural for them to want to look out for her.

"Since when did you not give two shits about Eva? You suddenly don't care what happens to her?"

"Maybe I care *too* much," he snapped.

"What the fuck is that supposed to mean?

"It means nothing," said North. "Forget it."

Colton stepped on the bottom rung of the ladder

leading up to the loft. He gave his brother a shove to garner his attention. "Something happen between the two of you?"

"Like what, Colt? I'm not an asshole, alright."

He slowly exhaled his breath. He'd worried about his day, wondered if it would ever come. It seemed the more North was hurt at home, the harder he'd hold onto Eva. It was an unhealthy cycle, but one he couldn't resist himself. Now his twin was starting to question his feelings, but he couldn't.

"You know Eva's something special. She's different than us. She comes from a good family and—"

"Don't!"

"I'm just saying...We have that bastard's blood running through our veins. What the fuck could we offer a girl like Eva? You want her ending up like ma, popping pills to forget the pain?"

"I'd never hurt her!" North leapt down from bed and began to pace the tiny trailer liked a caged panther.

"You think that now, but we're both holding onto too much baggage. One day it's bound to come rushing to the surface, and I for one don't want Eva around when it does."

North crossed his arms over his chest, staring out into the fields. "I'm not like him," he whispered.

"I know that, you know that, but is this really what you think is best for her?"

He watched his brother's jaw clench. Colton could feel the war playing inside him because he'd battled the same feelings before. He'd decided it was best to leave Eva untouched, as if protecting her virtue could undo all the wrongs he'd committed. Maybe if that one element of his life remained pure, it would balance out all the nasty shit he had to deal with on a daily basis. North needed to come to the same realization.

"Let's just find her before it gets dark," North said. "I'm done talking."

They set out on foot, watching the remaining crowds disperse towards the parking areas. His intuition led him to the Bronco riding event, and sure enough, he spotted Eva and Wade. Just looking at the cowboy made his anger flare. He clenched and unclenched his fists, attempting to maintain some semblance of control.

As they got closer, he could hear Eva's laughter. It was the sound that kept him sane too many times to count. When he'd seek her out after an especially bad day at home, her sweet innocence chased away his demons. He didn't want Wade sharing a minute of that sound.

"This what you expect to find?" asked North.

They both stopped dead before being spotted.

"Suppose it is." Colton ran a hand through his hair and took a deep breath in an attempt to douse his rising frustration. All he could envision was his fist contacting Wade's face.

He debated what his next move should be. North was acting out of character so he had to make the decision on his own. The natural thing to do would be to chase away Wade and get Eva to the safety of the silver bullet. But to what end? Like Eva said, she wasn't getting any younger and wanted to find herself a husband. But no man would ever be good enough for her in Colton's eyes, and there was no way in hell *he* was worthy of her attention.

When the couple leaned in close, every muscle in Colton's body turned stiff. Their proximity had a direct effect on his mood...and sanity. His earlier indecision was resolved for him when Wade kissed Eva. He swore a fucking floodgate of fury broke free inside him. North kept pace beside him as he stormed toward the rail fence where Eva sat with the cowboy.

"There you are," he called out before Wade could strike again.

Eva looked like a child caught with her hand in the cookie jar. Then she grew bold and narrowed her eyes at him. He knew that face. She was ready to ream him out for being overprotective. Colton wasn't sure what the fuck his role was any more. It seemed somewhere along the line Eva grew up without him even noticing. Now she was a woman and a damn fine one at that.

"Why are you looking for me? I don't need a babysitter."

"We expected you home hours ago," said Colton. "With all the scumbags prowling these rodeos, we thought we better save you."

"I don't need saving! Go home, both of you!"

She turned to Wade with a look of apology in her eyes.

"Eva, we ain't leaving you here," said North, suddenly showing his usual protective nature.

"Wade will bring me home later. You don't have to worry about me. Not one bit." She scowled at him with enough venom to make most men cower, and then shifted her body to face the cowboy, effectively cutting them off.

He grabbed North's shirt and started to walk away. What was he supposed to do? Make a scene for half the rodeo? Normally nothing would stop him, but then again, Eva had never shown such genuine interest in another man. For some reason it struck Colton the wrong way. Maybe the introduction of a love interest would deem Colton and his brother irrelevant. He needed her, and even though she wasn't his woman, he still didn't want to share.

"Where you going?" asked North, continually looking back over his shoulder. "Fine, I take it back, I do give a damn. Now let's go back and get her."

Colton shook his head. "There's no point. She's made her mind in the matter. If she wants that cowboy, more power to her."

"You trust that piece of shit? Did you see him kiss her?"

"It was just a kiss. Maybe he's Prince Charming. I don't know." Colton had no right to steal any happiness from Eva. She'd been his rock since his dad walked out on them. Without her, he'd never have made it through in one piece. Now she was old enough to move on with her life, to start a new generation of Fords. For years, he'd protected her, coddled her, and kept men at bay. Now she was a beautiful twenty-two-year-old woman ready to spread her wings.

"He sure as hell ain't Prince Charming!" North shrugged him off when Colton attempted to steer him towards the trailer.

"As long as she's home before dark, it's her life to live."

****

North was ready to brawl. In fact, he craved it like never before. Pain would be preferable to the ache in his heart. Somewhere along the line he began to see Eva as more than the sweet girl next door. Somewhere along the line he'd fallen in love.

What he didn't understand was Colton's sudden disinterest. Their feelings for Eva always mirrored each other's. Half the time when he'd escape to the Ford house, Colton was already there. They'd come on the trip specifically to keep Eva out of trouble, but instead, his twin was turning a blind eye.

They ate dinner in silence. North watched the sky

turn from blue to black, every darkening shade bringing his anxiety to a new level. She still wasn't back. God knows what that cowboy was doing with little Eva. The thought of his filthy hands on her made his blood boil. He wasn't sure how much longer he could sit still with his imagination running wild.

He was just about to bolt from his seat when the door to the trailer opened. Cool air flooded the interior and the sound of Eva clearing her throat made every live wire inside him suddenly lose power. He exhaled a nervous breath, glad she was at least home safely.

"Told you I'd be back in one piece," she said as she hung up her cardigan. "There's no need to go hunting me down. Seriously."

She started to climb up into the loft.

"Where's lover boy?" asked North, no humor in his tone.

"His name is Wade, and he just dropped me off, like a perfect gentleman."

"That why he had his lips all over you?" asked Colton. His brother was just as unimpressed, even though he'd condoned the behavior.

"Hush you!" Eva slipped under the covers.

"You haven't eaten," said North.

"Wade bought me dinner."

He ground his teeth together, stifling a growl. The sound of that man's name on Eva's lips made him see red. If he never heard the name again it would be too soon.

They secured the trailer and turned out the lights before joining Eva in the bed. He tossed his shirt and lay down on his back, staring up at the low ceiling. She was already comfortable, obviously not feeling the volatile energy keeping him awake. He kept as far to his side as possible, the cold wall of the trailer chilling his arm.

Every time she shifted in the bed, he tensed.

"I'm cold," she murmured, cuddling closer to him. The heat of her body scorched his bare skin. In a matter of days, everything changed for him. He wasn't sure when it happened, but he wished he could go back to the way things were. Uncomplicated.

He tried to get away from her but he was trapped in the tight confines of the sleeping area. He held his breath as she ran her palm over his chest, over and over in small circles. Her touch had always been soothing—not so much anymore.

"What's wrong with you?" she whispered against his neck. His eyes lolled back in his head. Even her fucking breath was sweet.

"Nothing. Go to sleep, Eva."

"You're acting weird, North. Is this because of Wade?"

He decided the cowboy was a safer topic than his changing feelings for her. "I don't trust him."

"Why not?"

"Just don't is all." He rolled to his side and away from her. It didn't feel right going to sleep on a sour note, but he couldn't have this discussion now. Mrs. Ford was the one to teach him and Colton not to speak out of passion. It was always best to confront a person with a level head, after cooling off and replaying the events over in your head. He usually didn't take the advice, but tonight felt like a good time to start.

"Will you two quiet down," said Colton.

Eva pressed her body against his back. Why had he taken off his shirt? He needed layers between them—many, many layers.

"I know what I'm doing," she said in a whisper. "You don't have to worry about me."

"I'd worry less if you spent more time with

Bessie and Ruby than that drifter."

"He's not a drifter."

"Why you defending him?" he asked. "You act like you're already an item."

She kissed his shoulder. "I just want you to be happy for me, North."

"It doesn't matter what I think."

"It does. You're the one who taught me how to rope a calf, and even though it took me weeks to learn, you never got impatient. You protected me when Jameson's dogs got loose." She ran her hand delicately down his arm, her fingers lingering over the raised scars on his forearm. "You bought me a corsage when no boy asked me to prom. Remember when the three of us danced in the rain that night? My dress was covered in mud."

"I remember."

"Well those are just examples of why I love you so much. It doesn't feel right doing anything without your blessing."

He wasn't sure he could ever give her what she wanted.

Chapter Six

The following afternoon, Eva went to take care of Bessie and Ruby. She needed to keep up their appearances because the judges would be in town tomorrow morning. Wade was waiting for her in the holding paddock, his hat in his hand as he leaned over the rails. They usually spent time together before she got to work and he had to go practice, but this was the first time the McReed brothers knew about it. They'd walked her to the barn today, and when she looked back over her shoulder, they were both still standing on the periphery. Colton and North looked like hired guards with their arms crossed over their chests.

She didn't want to disappoint them, in the same way she never wanted to disappoint her father. Their opinions mattered, but she had the idea no man would ever be good enough in their eyes. It was the reason she was taking the reins of her own future.

"Good afternoon, darlin'." Wade brushed some stray hairs from her face, a lazy smile on his lips.

"Hi." Her stomach felt sour knowing the twins were watching and disapproving. When she dared to peek behind her, they were gone. She sighed in relief and turned to focus on Wade.

"You alright?"

"I'm fine now. Are we still on for tonight?" she asked.

He worried his lip. "About that, baby doll, I'll have to postpone. I'm meeting with one of those sponsors from the city tonight. It came up sudden like."

"Don't worry about it. It sounds like it may be a good opportunity for you," she said.

"That's what I'm hoping."

She stayed with Wade for twenty minutes before he had to leave for a barrel racing event. Eva collected her grooming supplies and slipped in the stall with Bessie and Ruby. She began to slowly rub circles over Ruby's coat with the curry comb. Her mind was elsewhere.

What had she really come to Chester for? She'd been seeking something—excitement, freedom, success, love? She wasn't so sure. Wade was handsome and attentive, but she'd be lying if she said he made her heart pitter patter. She thought true love would hit her like a firestorm and whisk off her feet. Instead she felt out of place, trying to create something out of nothing. If she returned home without a ribbon or a man to show for her trip, she'd feel like a failure. If she could bring home a cowboy to make her daddy proud, it would be the beginning of a new and better life for her. Or so she believed.

After returning home from the barn, the silver bullet was empty. There was no sign of the twins, only the faint scent of Colt's musky cologne. In fact, she spent most of the evening alone, no clue where to find Colton or North. It was odd not having them breathing down her neck every minute. It was nice, but in a weird way, she missed their constant meddling.

****

Colton waited for North in front of the local pub. He was late. It was nearing dinner hour, so the place was filling up in a hurry.

When his brother finally made an appearance, he looked worse than shit.

"Where've you been so long?"

"I told you I was hauling hay," said North. He took off his Stetson and swatted some of the dust off his jeans.

"That shouldn't have taken this long."

"They asked me to set up a roadblock and make a wall around the petting zoo. Not many of their hired workers can move hay with a forklift." North shrugged. "It was worth it. I wanted us to have enough money to take Eva to dinner tomorrow night. She likes stuff like that."

Colton scowled. His brother was acting like a schoolboy in love. "How do you know?"

"Didn't you hear her voice when she mentioned Wade took her out to dinner? She ain't used to stuff like that, and she deserves it."

"Let's get a drink." Colton pushed open the heavy wooden door and entered the melee. The place was already packed, and they had to weave their way to the back bar.

He ordered a couple shots for both of them. Colton wanted to forget the world as much as he needed to stay away from alcohol. It was too similar to the nightmare his mother was putting them through, and it all stemmed back to that one asshole. He swallowed his first shot, trying to envision Jess McReed walking into the bar. Colton wasn't a scared kid anymore, ready to cower under the sight of his belt or fist. He was a grown man, and his father would be a fool to land a hand on him today.

He swirled the dark amber liquid around the second glass, staring at it as he lost himself in his fantasy world. It seemed everything was falling apart around him. He couldn't help himself, never mind his mother or his twin. His only escape was slipping away like water through his fingers. Any time now and Eva would walk out of his life just like his father did. He thought the pain twelve years ago was unbearable. Losing Eva wouldn't even compare.

"Set me up again," he said to the barkeep.

"Take it easy," said North. "You'll regret it come morning."

Colt choked back more throat-burning whiskey before turning to face the crowd, his elbows resting on the bar. "Is that who I think it is?"

Even with a good buzz building up, he recognized Wade sitting at a table near the entrance. He didn't even hesitate to march over to the piece of shit.

North pulled out a chair and sat backwards on it, inviting himself to the party of two. "You have good taste in women, Wade." His brother's tone was anything but friendly.

The cowboy wasn't fazed. "Just a friend, boys." He nodded to the buckle bunny to leave, smacking her ass as she sauntered off. "How's your sister doing, anyway?"

"She's not our sister, and I imagine she's off dreaming about you right now." Colton was seriously pissed off. As much as he hated the cowboy for stealing Eva's heart away from him, he wanted the best for her. He wanted her happy.

"Look, it's not going to work out, okay." Wade tipped his beer bottle back for a drink. He acted as if he was talking about the weather.

"What the hell not? She's fucking gorgeous. You'd never find a finer woman that her."

"Exactly. I'm not looking for a wife. She's lucky I waited on her as long as I did, but a peck on the cheek after nearly a week isn't going to cut it."

"You're a filthy bastard," said North. His tossed the chair to the side when he stood. "What gives you the right to play with Eva's heart?"

He shrugged. "Her mother should have taught her about men like me."

Colton's blood was boiling. "She never had to

worry because she had us. I shouldn't have let down my guards, especially when you rubbed me wrong from day one."

He wanted to fight. The alcohol only spurred him on, pushing him to take chances.

"Let's go," said North. "I'm done with this."

If it wasn't for his twin, he'd be rolling with Wade about now, determined to teach him what happens to men that break Eva's heart.

He pushed his brother when he wouldn't stop dragged him away by the shirt. Colton hadn't realized he was digging his heels against the floor.

"You're already wasted, Colt. For God's sake!"

"Don't judge me. You don't know what I'm going through." He unbuttoned the top buttons of his shirt, the heat rising up his collar.

"Who the fuck do you think I am? I know everything. You've been feeling sorry for yourself ever since dad walked out on us."

Colton didn't think, he just acted. He threw a punch at his brother's face, all the rage building inside him desperate to be expelled. "We have no dad!"

North grabbed his wrist and punched him hard in the gut. Colton bent forward to catch his breath. They fought back and forth, throwing punching, grabbing, and ramming each other without holding back. A bubble of space grew around them. The patrons of the bar hooted and hollered for bloodshed. Little did they know North was his brother and best friend.

"Whatever. Move on. Or am I a fucking reminder to you, too?"

North's words sobered Colton in a hurry. His brother was going through the same, if not more, pain as him. Their mother couldn't even look at him when she was high.

They settled into chairs at an empty table, and within minutes, the music resumed and the crowd forgot about them.

"You've looked better," said Colton.

North smirked. "You should have seen the other guy."

He ordered a coffee, not willing to head back to the trailer in a drunken stupor. His lip was split and his ribs ached, but he deserved it.

"How are we gonna tell Eva?" asked North.

"The hell if I know." He sipped on his coffee, noticing some girls at the bar checking out their table.

"I didn't like seeing her with him."

He shrugged. "It'll happen one day, North. Maybe not with Wade, but with another man."

"Why not us?"

Colton tensed. "Don't start. You know she deserves better than us."

"Like Wade? I'd never cheat on her, never do anything to hurt her."

"I ain't having this conversation," said Colton.

All he could envision was Eva popping pills like their mother because he was destined to follow in his father's footsteps. He wouldn't ruin her.

"So I have to pretend I feel nothing?"

A couple of women from the bar walked over. One handed a beer to North. "Hey, big boy."

"You just need to move on," said Colton, patting his lap. He'd just do what he did best—stifle the pain, put on a happy face, and love Eva like he always had.

****

Eva was about to crawl into bed but knew she wouldn't be able to sleep. Where were Colton and North? It was way past dark, so they could only be at one place. Neither of them had chased tail like she expected since arriving, so she assumed they were at the local bar. She was tempted to go look for them, but their social life was none of her business, especially when she continually ranted for them to stay out of hers.

She tidied up the clothes left in the sleeping area and cleaned the kitchen, but she couldn't get the twins off her mind. What if they'd gotten themselves into trouble? It wouldn't be the first time. Eva finally decided to take a walk around the campgrounds to see if she could spot either of them. She pulled on a warm sweater and slipped on her boots.

Rain fell in a light mist, and the only light came from the Chinese lanterns and bonfires. She hugged herself tighter as she walked to the first trailer. A middle-aged woman was warming her hands by the fire.

"Hi, have you seen the men I'm rooming with lately? They still aren't home, and I was getting a bit worried."

"Haven't seen either of your brothers, sugar. The blond one was by earlier. He fixed my trailer hitch and carried my groceries into the kitchen. Handsome as hell *and* sweet. If I were younger, I'd be chasing both of them." She laughed out loud and pulled out a beer bottle from the side of her chair. "Go check the pub. You'll probably find them there."

Eva didn't 'want people mistaking the twins as her brothers. It never bothered her before, but it rubbed her wrong now. She came to the next campsite, stopping to speak to three cowgirls drinking and talking.

"Have any of you seen Colton or North? The men I'm bunking with?"

One of them whispered into another's ear. They giggled. The third was bolder. "No, but if you find either of them cowboys, send them to me." She winked.

Eva never had a possessive bone in her body. She

loved the McReed twins as much as her own soul. They were a huge part of her life. However, she also accepted they slept around and would eventually have families of their own.

A new fear sparked inside her. What if they did move on without her? Could she really stand to see them in love with another woman?

"Thanks. I'll keep looking."

Eva started to jog through the campsites, half in a daze. She'd been blind her entire adult life. How could she not see what was right in front of her?

She burst into the bar as soon as she reached it. Eva wasn't sure what she was going to do or say when she found Colton and North, but she had to find them. She breathlessly pushed through the throngs of people. The country music drowned all the multitude of conversations. Cowboys looked her up and down as she squeezed by, but she ignored everyone around her. When she finally spotted the twins, she stopped dead in her tracks.

They were both sitting at a table with two scantily clad women. The blonde had enough cleavage for half the bar, and the brunette was planting kisses on North's neck. Eva couldn't breathe. She came to Chester expecting the guys to have their fun. She never loved them in more than a platonic way. They were the McReed boys, her neighbors, the teens who pestered her, and the men who became her rocks in life. God, she was such a fool.

She stepped closer, wondering if it was too late to change…everything.

Eva was standing right beside their table, looking down at them. It was Colt who finally noticed a person standing there. He did a double take but didn't push his date away. Eva had to remember that nothing had changed in their heads, and they'd done nothing wrong.

"Why you out at this hour?" he asked.

She desperately wanted to replicate disinterest, to appear unfazed by the beautiful women hanging off them. All it would take was a simple comment about being bored or curious. But the lies stayed lodged in her throat.

Eva opened her mouth to speak but nothing came out. Her new emotions came rushing to the surface, threatening her to break down in tears and make a fool of herself. She turned and bolted towards the exit without a word. The fresh, cool night air was a relief from the stuffy interior of the bar. All she knew was she had to get away, to hide, to think. The brothers probably thought she'd lost her ever-loving mind. How would she explain herself?

She started running back to the silver bullet, tears blurring her vision. She was about to ruin two perfect friendships. Life without Colton and North would be unbearable—she couldn't even imagine a day without them underfoot.

The rain picked up, falling in heavy sheets. She nearly slipped a few times on the slick paths, reminded of their day at the pig wrangling event. Eva cried harder, imagining those bimbos stealing what she loved.

Eva only made it to the rear of the large barn with the outdoor showers. It was difficult to see with only the odd overhead light in the event areas. It was like a ghost town this far from the campground. She could see the strength of the rain in the lamp light when she stopped to catch her breath.

"Eva!" It was North's voice. She wished they'd given her some space, but then again, it would be unlike them not to chase after her. At least some things hadn't changed. She'd tell them she was sick, her stomach doing flips. It would explain her refusal to answer Colton and her sudden disappearing act.

Colton called out over the static of rainfall, "Eva wait up!"

Why wasn't she stopping? Why did her tears keep falling? She was conflicted on a soul deep level. Everything had always been simple and pure between them. Now she was thinking beyond what they shared when she should be satisfied with the way things were.

A hand wrapped around her upper arm, jolting her to a standstill. "Didn't you hear me calling?" asked North.

She refused to look him in the face. Eva didn't look beautiful when she cried. Her eyes got puffy and her skin broke out into hives. There would be no way to conceal her turbulent emotions.

"Leave me be," she said. "Please."

North's jeans were soaked to the skin. She'd never noticed the shiny silver buckle he wore. Eva realized she'd never paid attention to their physical appearances, as if she went through life with blinders on. Now she really looked—strong thighs, narrow hips, and massive muscular frames.

"Eva, what in God's name are you thinking?" Colton stopped talking to catch his breath.

"Just go back to the bar. Your dates are probably worried sick." She couldn't hide the note of resentment in her tone, and she was supposed to try and play this night off.

"They're not our dates," said North, tilting her chin up to face him. "Why are you crying?"

Water ran in rivulets from his soaked hair. His lips were moist and thick, his eyes dark and piercing. How could she have been so blind?

"I'm not."

He chuckled, not releasing her face. "That's insulting, Eva. I think I know you better than that."

She shook her head and shrugged him off. As she attempted to rush away into the darkness, Colt grabbed her around the waist and held her in place. "No more running, little one."

"I can't do this," she cried. "I've messed up bad. I need time to clear my head."

"What happened?" asked North. "Was it Wade? He say something to you?"

"I'll kill him," Colt whispered in her ear. His breath smelled of alcohol. He held her tighter, her back pressed to his chest.

"It wasn't Wade!" She struggled in his arms. "It was me."

"Mrs. Ford's the one always telling us it's never as bad as it seems." North brushed the matted hair off her cheeks and ran his thumb along her lower lip. The simple gestures never aroused her before, but now her stomach fluttered wildly, and her heart pumped so fast she could scarcely breathe.

"This is worse."

North's shirt was plastered to his body from the rain. It seemed every muscle was accentuated from his broad shoulders to his massive biceps. She stared blankly, new erotic thoughts swirling in her head. The struggle inside her didn't let up. Her chest jerked erratically from crying too hard.

"Tell me what's wrong with you, God dammit!"

"I fell in love."

Chapter Seven

North took a step back and nearly fell on his ass. He wiped the rain from his eyes, staring back at Eva while his heart crumbled to pieces. She was in love with Wade, and even though he knew there was no future for the two of them, it didn't hurt any less. Colton was right—it was better when he didn't care.

"There's nothing wrong with that."

"There is," she whispered. "When it's you."

North froze, staring at her as if seeing her for the first time. He reacted on instinct, cupping her face with both hands as he kissed her hard on the lips. The rain and her feminine taste intermingled. He kissed her long and deep, exactly how he'd envisioned. She was so soft and sweet and perfect.

When he finally pulled back, her lips were parted and swollen. Colt had moved beside him. "You love North?"

"And you," she said. "I love you both."

North wasn't surprised or offended. He'd always been one with his twin. Most of his time shared with Eva included Colton in some degree. It was the new revelation that shocked him. He'd been battling his own budding feelings for the Ford girl. To hear they were reciprocated made everything right with his world.

"You don't know what you're saying, baby doll," said Colton. "We're no good for you."

What was Colton doing? Their sweet girl just admitted to loving them, and he was already trying to push her away.

North kissed her again when she tried to speak. "Don't listen to him. He's drunk."

"I'm so sorry," she murmured. "I don't want to

lose either of you."

"I've always loved you. That will never change."

This time she touched his face, her delicate fingers traced around his eye and along his jaw. It felt so damned good. "I was jealous."

North smirked. "You never need to be jealous, Eva. I'm yours."

She exhaled in a rush before reaching her arms up around his neck. "*Yes,*" she whispered. The little thing pressed her body against his. She'd done it a million times when they hugged, but not like this. His cock stirred to life, his entire body taut as he tried to behave.

There was something magical in the air enhanced by the rain and darkness.

"I love you so much," he muttered against her neck. She smelled sweet, like strawberries and cream.

"You'll catch your death of a cold out here, Eva. Your mother will kill us for not taking better care of you," said Colton. His twin separated them, leading Eva towards the trailer by holding her bent elbow. They all moved in silence, not saying a word during the long walk, but there were so many things running in his head. North was processing all the possibilities, and he still wasn't one hundred percent convinced he wasn't dreaming.

Once safely inside the silver bullet, the rain and dampness shut out, Colton pinned Eva against the living room wall. "What am I going to do with you, little lady?"

She looked up at him, her sweet faced framed by her dripping wet hair. "Love me back?"

He shook his head. "I can't give you something you already have."

"Kiss me then."

Colt held back, staring at her with an arm braced at either side of her head. "I can't." He spun around, massaging behind his neck. Why couldn't he just accept the gift she offered? Why did Colton always have to make things difficult?

North didn't want Eva upset. He moved in and began to peel off her heavily soaked sweater. "You can't stay in these wet clothes," he said.

She nodded, but he'd already seen the hurt Colt left in her eyes. He tossed the damp material in the corner and didn't know where to go next. Her shirt clung to her curves and the girl didn't even have on a bra. He tried to look away—and failed.

"You look real good," he whispered. North leaned over and kissed the smooth plane of her neck. She was the ultimate temptation. He slipped his hands under the bottom edge of her shirt and moved up. Her skin was chilled and breaking out in gooseflesh. He could feel her stomach quiver as his rough hands moved up her soft sides. North slowly kissed his way to her lips. She was ready and eager, parting her lips for his tongue. They kissed with such passion, he never wanted to stop. By the time his hands reached the bottom edge of her breasts, Colt pulled him back by the shoulder.

North was getting tired of his brother. "What the fuck?"

"Eva go get changed in the loft," Colt said. She listened, slipping away and climbing up onto the bed. His twin stared him down.

"What is up with you?"

"You're taking advantage of her, North. You need to keep your hands to yourself."

He wouldn't be denied the one thing he wanted most. North bent forward and charged into Colt, ramming him into the other wall. The entire trailer rocked back and forth as they slammed each other from side to side. "I'd never take advantage of her!"

"She's not yours." Colton punctuated his words with a sharp punch to the gut.

"Then she sure as hell ain't yours, Colt."

North managed to rip his brother's shirt off over his head, before kneeing him in the ribs. They were about to lunge forward again, but they were stopped by Eva's voice.

"Stop it! You're both being ridiculous," she shouted. "Now stop upsetting me and come to bed."

North exhaled and he could see Colt visibly lose his steam. They were both too hardwired to make Eva happy. He flicked off the lights and started to climb into bed. Colton went to the bathroom.

"Not with those wet clothes. Take them off before you wet all the blankets."

He complied since the trailer was in shadows. North kicked off his clammy jeans and lost his shirt. He crawled into the loft and dropped down on his side. His skin was chilled, but he felt anything but cold next to Eva.

"Where's Colt?"

"He's coming in a minute."

"I'm cold," she said. "Warm me up." Eva slipped under his blanket, skin to skin. She wore nothing at all. His Herculean control was shot down the moment of physical contact.

She rested her cheek against his chest, and he could feel her little nipple pebbled against his side. "How do I make you feel?" she whispered.

"What do you mean?"

"Do I make you feel as good as those women in the bar?"

He huffed. "Much better."

"We always talk about everything back home. Why not now? Why do things have to change?"

He took a cleansing breath. "What do you want to know?"

"Do I turn you on?"

She was playing with fire and didn't even realize it. "Yes."

"Tell me how it feels." Eva ran her palm over the roundness of his shoulder, her fingers testing the strength of his biceps.

"You make my dick hard."

She kissed his chest, her little tongue flicking out to taste him. Her hand slid lower and lower. North swallowed hard. When her hand rubbed over the top of his damp boxer briefs, her reached down and grabbed her wrist.

"Why can't I touch you?" she asked.

"Because you just can't do that and not expect me to…react."

"Tell me," she said, her hand returning to his chest. "How do you want to react?"

"Eva, stop it."

"Tell me," she insisted. "You said I make you hard. Then what?"

He had to control his fucking breathing just to speak. Never had a woman had such a pull over him. North rolled over so he dominated, pinning her under him. "I want to fuck you, to fill your sweet little virgin pussy with my cock."

"Oh God," she whimpered, pulling him down to her lips. She kissed him, nipping and sucking in between gasping for air.

"North!" Colton's loud baritone filled the trailer.

"Colton McReed stop being dumb and come to bed," said Eva. She wouldn't let North go, returning to their kiss. Her desire was like a living force, calling to him like a siren.

As Colt climbed up, he shoved North to his side, inadvertently tossing the blankets as well. Eva lay on the bed completely nude. Her body was perfect and youthful, her breasts soft, tempting swells, and her hips beautifully rounded.

"Please kiss me, Colt." She reached up to him, beckoning him to lower over her body. "*Please*."

Colton didn't say a word. He lowered over her body, careful to hover out of contact. Eva grabbed him around the neck and pulled him down. His brother resisted at first but finally accepted Eva when she kissed him first.

"More," she whined. "Touch me."

****

Colton wanted to keep his distance but how could he resist Eva when she begged him to kiss her? What harm could it do now that North had crossed the line?

He kissed Eva Ford. His heart screamed out that she was *his* girl, but he knew a life with him would go nowhere fast. The one kiss quickly turned into much more when she began to squirm beneath him, thrusting her hips to get closer. She was ripe, but he wouldn't pick her. Not little Eva.

"I'm hot all over," she said. "You know how to make it better, Colt."

Eva knew they'd had their fair share of fast women over the years. They meant nothing. Eva meant everything.

Her fucking hands smoothed over his back, holding him close. When she parted her thighs, he dropped down against her center. He was still in his jeans and his cock was about to blow off the zipper. "Stop teasing, Eva."

"I'm not." She nipped and sucked his shoulder. Her little mewling sounds drove him crazy. "Stop being cruel. I thought you loved me."

Shit. Eva was able to play with his heart strings effortlessly. He shifted to his side of the bed, leaving her on her back in the middle. Colton ran the backs of his fingers along her parted inner thighs. She tried to turn and face him, but he stilled her with a palm to the stomach.

He travelled straight to her center, cupping her mound and the neat patch of dark-blonde curls. She gasped and began to pant in anticipation. The Ford girl was the essence of innocence, experiencing everything for the first time. He wanted it to be perfect for her.

North moved in, drawn in by Eva's wanton desire. It was nearly palpable. He descended on her pert little tit, suckling the nipple into his mouth. She grabbed onto his head to hold him into place.

"That feels so good, North. Oh my God."

Colton pushed the limit, penetrating her wet pussy with two fingers. Her breath caught. She attempted to close her legs, by decided to drop them open at the knees instead. He slowly began to finger-fuck her, careful not to push too deep. With just the right curl of his fingers, he'd help her achieve an orgasm within minutes.

North alternated between her breasts and her lips. The scent of sex perfumed the air. When Colton added the precise pressure to her G-spot, it pushed her over the edge. Eva cried out, clutching at both of them. She was like a ship without an anchor, and Colt wanted to be the one to teach her everything. He kept his fingers inside her, eager to feel her tight inner walls milk him, imagining it was his cock.

"Let it all go, baby girl."

When she finally calmed down, her breathing coming in a regular pattern, he covered her with the blankets.

"That was incredible," she said.

He couldn't count the number of times they'd all slept together in Eva's room. Colton had never been tempted to cross a line. Now the lines were blurred, and for the first time he could see the lure of forever.

Chapter Eight

It was the day of the judging. Eva wasn't surprised the brothers were gone when she woke up. She'd been worried things would be uncomfortable after everything they'd shared last night. Her only regret was the fact they refused to take things all the way. As soon as she'd smartened up and accepted what was in front of her all along, there was no going back. She loved Colton and North unconditionally, flaws and all.

She tugged on her jeans, the snug denim making her pussy pulse. Eva stopped to catch her breath. It only took one memory of last night to make her feel that same wanton energy. The McReed twins felt so good, all hard and muscly. They were strong and attentive, holding back because they loved her. She trusted them completely and wanted so much more from them.

Eva set out for the holding paddock. She needed to get Bessie and Ruby in top form. This was the day she'd been waiting for. As she walked along the beaten paths, she realized the sky seemed bluer, the grass greener. Her eyes had been opened to a new world. She felt complete, like she'd finally finished a twenty-two-year-old puzzle.

When she spotted Wade waiting for her by the split rail fence, she cursed under her breath. She'd forgotten all about him. He'd made her feel good because he was the first man to pay attention to her. He symbolized freedom and the adult life she'd always sought. But never once was she foolish enough to believe it was love.

"Good morning, pretty lady."

She smiled as she approached. "Hi, Wade."

"Today's the big day, is it?"

Eva nodded. She looked to the side where the cows were kept, wondering how she could tell him things would never work between them.

"I wanted to show you something. I'm packing up tonight and heading on the road, so this is my last chance."

If that were true, she'd be free of any ties. The least she could do was see what he wanted to show her. "Okay, but I can't be long. The judges will be doing a walk through soon."

"It won't take long." He smiled and then led her away by the small of the back. They followed a narrow path behind the barn. It was a downward slope moving away from the events to a series of small outbuildings. She wondered if he was going to show her the new foals she'd heard talk of. Baby animals were always a weakness of hers. She'd personally brought at least a dozen calves into the world on their farm.

She looked around when they reached the bottom of the hill. It was odd there weren't any cowboys or hired hands around. Eva began to feel uneasy, especially when Wade kept mentioning how beautiful she looked.

"So, who are those boys you're bunking with exactly?"

She was tongue-tied for a moment. "They're my friends from the next ranch over. I've known them since I was a little girl."

"But you're not a little girl anymore, are you? You look very much like a woman to me."

Eva swallowed hard, staring at the path they'd just taken. Should she run? Or was she just overreacting? "Thank you," she whispered.

He backed her up until she hit the side of a small wooden shed. It hid their view from every angle but the dense forest behind them. "I've invested a lot of time in you, Eva. Don't you think I should be rewarded?"

She narrowed her eyes, not understanding his meaning. "I thought you were going to show me something."

"I plan to, darlin'." He reached down and began to fiddle with the buckle on his leather belt. She glanced down and couldn't believe what was happening. Her father was the essence of an old-fashioned cowboy. Honor, loyalty, and his word meant everything. She couldn't even remember a day he'd raised his voice at her mother.

Wade may have bragging rights in the ring, but he was no gentleman. Adrenaline spiked through her veins. For once, she wished the overbearing McReed brothers were there to pound Wade into the earth.

"What are you doing?"

He tried to kiss her neck, but she turned away in distaste. "Stop playing hard to get. Do you realize how many women I've turned down this week for you?"

"I'm sorry you expected more, but I'm not interested."

He laughed without humor. "Too late for that. You can't expect to tease a man and walk away."

"I need to go," she said, pushing him back. He clasped her wrists in one hand and refused to let her leave.

"Didn't I make myself clear?" His words were angry, his face changing into something new and terrifying. "You're not leaving until you pay up. Either open your legs or suck my dick, either way is fine by me."

****

"You get a hold of her?" asked North.

Colton shook his head. "Second day with no answer. I hope Aunt Laura remembered to stop by."

"It's a good thing we're heading home tomorrow."

Their mother may be a grown woman, but she was incapable of taking care of herself with an addiction ruling her life. No matter how cruel she was to him these days, North still worried about her.

"There's nothing we can do now. We might as well head to the judging," said North.

They'd both been avoiding Eva like the plague. They fought to be the first one out of bed and out the door in the morning. North was a fucking mess. It was nerve-wracking wondering if Eva regretted their night of passionate confessions. Would she play it off? Hate them? Resent them? He felt like a bastard for taking anything she'd offered. She was innocent, reacting to the raw lust between them. Or was it really love?

He wouldn't be able to handle a rejection from Eva. It would destroy Colt. After their dad walked away, his twin focused all those feelings of abandonment on Eva Ford. She was his rock, and it seemed they both needed her as much as air.

"Maybe we should wait a while. I don't think the judges will be by until the afternoon," said Colt.

"We have to face her sooner or later."

"I don't think I can. Last night I lost control. I never should have given in like I did. She probably hates me."

North smirked. "She was offering, but you didn't take, Colt. She'll know that."

His brother ran both hands through his mess of dirty-blond hair. "This is crazy, you do realize that?"

"Since when has our family ever been normal?"

They walked along the path, careful not to speak too loudly. The event grounds were bustling with people, horses being walked by, and vendors calling out their wares.

"What about Mr. Ford?" asked Colt, his voice sober. "I don't think I could take it if he shut me out."

"I love him, too," said North. "But I also love Eva."

"I'm not as simple as love. Even if he approved, he'd expect one of us, not both."

North didn't want to think about tomorrow or the consequences. He was too high on love, too overjoyed since Eva revealed her feelings. The sobering reality of a ménage à trois relationship was one he'd consider—later.

"I'm done talking. I need Eva." Just like back home, she was always the answer.

The holding paddock for the cattle was crowded with spectators. How were they supposed to find Eva in that mess?

"I hope they haven't started the judging," said Colt.

"No, they're just getting ready." He walked up to judging table where several employees he recognized were chatting. "Afternooon." North tilted his Stetson in greeting. "Have ya'll seen Eva around? Looks like Bessie and Ruby are still in the holding pen."

"I'm not sure, sugar," said Patsy, one of the event planners. "I was wondering where she was myself. There's not much time left to prepare."

He looked at his brother. Neither of them said a word.

A hired hand raking hay a few feet away spoke up. "She was here a while ago. Went down to the storage units with that Granger fellow."

"What Granger fellow?" asked North. His hackles were up, but he kept his cool.

"Wade Granger. I've seen him with Eva nearly every day this week. I'm sure they just wanted to be alone." Patsy winked. "But you might want to remind her that she needs to get back in a hurry."

"Where'd you see them heading?" asked Colton.

The hired hand pointed to the forest behind the main barn. North nudged Colt's shoulder and then took off jogging. They pushed their way unceremoniously through the crowds. Red lights flashed in his head. He had a bad feeling about this. After last night, he was certain Eva wouldn't want any type of intimacy with Wade. And after finding out the cowboy was a two-timer only looking for a quick fuck, he was terrified knowing Eva was alone with him.

"There's no way she'd miss preparing for the judging," said Colt as they ran down a grassy slope. It was slick from last night's rain, forcing them to slow down. There were numerous abandoned sheds in the near distance, most dilapidated and weather-beaten. He couldn't think of any good reason for Wade to bring Eva here.

"No shit."

North heard Eva's muffled scream when they neared the small wooden structures. They silently motioned to each other to split up and flank the bastard.

"Make your choice or I'll make it for you," said Wade.

When North peeked around the corner, the sight stole his humanity. His precious little Eva was pinned against the shed wall with Wade holding her against her will. He held her hands as she struggled to fend him off.

His fears dissipated. Although he hadn't stepped in yet, he wasn't worried about losing this fight. Eva's honor and safety were at stake. And Wade just made the worst decision of his life.

"Get your mother fucking hands off her," said Colt. His brother moved in from the other side of the shed. His features were set hard as stone, the promise of pain written in his eyes.

Wade took a step back and Eva immediately ran to North, wrapping her arms around his waist. He held her head to his chest, keeping her close. He never wanted to let her go.

"It's not what it looks like."

"It's exactly what it looks like," said Colton. He shoved Wade, nearly making him stumble. "You put your hands on my Eva."

"Men like you should be corralled and gelded," said North. "In the very least, you need to learn a lesson from someone your own size."

He hadn't been in as many fights as Colton over the years, but he could hold his own. North earned every one of his muscles through back-breaking hard work on the ranch. He was thankful for this strength on days like today.

"She can't just get away with leading a man on," said Wade. "I thought we understood each other last night."

"Eva can do whatever the fuck she wants," said North. Eva was an innocent country girl and Wade knew that. He had no right taking if she wasn't offering. After seeing the abuse his mother received from their father first-hand, he was sensitive to any woman being hurt by a man.

"Get her out of here." Colton may not have any championship trophies like Wade, but he'd been fighting dirty since he was a teen. It was usually because he was mad with the world, but it gave him the experience to deal with this asshole.

****

Eva felt all her fears drain from her body and settle in her boots. It was exhausting after being so stressed and frightened. She'd been used to her father, the McReed brothers, and the close-knit community in their small town. Wade forced her to see a side of humanity she'd never seen firsthand. She'd been humiliated and victimized and experienced a sense of helplessness she never wanted to relive. Eva came to Chester to gain her independence, not lose it.

North attempted to lead her away, but she dug her heels into the ground. "What about Colt?"

"He'll catch up in a minute." North scooped her up into his strong arms as if she weighed twenty pounds. After feeling so vulnerable, it felt amazing being sheltered by one of the men she loved. The McReed twins were her heroes and always would be.

The sound of punches being landed made her gasp. Wade and Colton were both hardcore cowboys, tall and solidly built. There was cursing and banging as they crashed into the small shed. North kept walking, not even worried about his brother.

"He could get hurt!" she said. "You have to help him."

North kissed her forehead. "Colton's teaching that piece of shit a lesson. I'd like to be in his boots right now."

"But—"

"But nothing. Tell me one thing, did he hurt you?"

She sighed. "No. I'm okay."

"Good thing because you have a ribbon to win."

Eva shook her head. "I can't. I'll be humiliated after what happened."

"Nobody knows a thing, little lady. I didn't come all the way to Chester for you to give up right before the finish line. You'll regret walking away."

He set her on her feet before they neared the

crowds. She had to get her thoughts together, to calm her nerves so she could do her job. Eva tried to convince herself she was being ridiculous. The McReed brothers came to her aid before Wade could really harm her. Then why did she feel so lost? Why were more tears threatening to fall? She'd foolishly trusted Wade, thrived on his courtship, and ignored the warnings by North and Colton.

She took a deep breath and slipped into the holding paddock, not making eye contact with any of the spectators or staff. Eva felt like she was an open book to the crowd, even though North was probably right, and nobody was the wiser.

Eva hugged Bessie, the familiar sight healing her a degree. She began to primp the cow as the other animals were being showed. The loudspeaker in the distance gave her a sense of urgency. Any minute and they'd call for Bessie or Ruby. She wouldn't let Wade steal all the excitement of this day. She'd been waiting for it for months, prepared for years, and wanted to savor every minute.

When she was finished grooming both girls, a low whistle caught her attention. Colt leaned over the rail of the holding pen and winked at her with a smile. "Good luck, baby girl."

She rushed over to him, touching the cut on his cheek. "You're hurt."

"I'm just fine. You worry about showing those prized cows. Tell Bessie she'll be steaks if she doesn't win."

He'd lifted her spirits, but she playfully swatted him anyway.

Her name was called, and she had to lead Bessie out first. She held her breath, convinced she'd screw something up. This wasn't just her first competition but also her first time in the city. Everything was new and unfamiliar. As she attempted to lead the cow out to the judging ring, the brat stalled, stubbornly fighting to stay put. Back at home, she handled the livestock with ease, but she froze under the stress of the moment. Colton leaned over and whacked Bessie on the rump. It was enough to get her moving.

This was going to be one week to remember.

Chapter Nine

That evening, they sat outside of their trailer to enjoy their last night away from home. Colton had a good bonfire blazing, the sparks dancing up into the sky. Eva sat on a bench with a quilt wrapped around her shoulders.

"So, how's it feel to be the owner of a prized cow?" he asked, sitting next to her.

Eva smiled. "She came in *third*."

"Hey, you have a blue ribbon. That's all that matters." He tucked some stray blonde hairs behind her ear. Colton had promised himself to keep his distance, but she needed him as much as he needed her. His sweet girl had been through the wringer because of that jerk. He needed to hear her laugh, to see the innocence in her eyes again.

North sat down on the other side of Eva. "You've been quiet tonight. You okay?"

She shrugged. "Still a bit shaken, I guess."

"Nobody will ever hurt you again," said North. "You're ours and we protect what's ours."

His brother made a weighty statement, one that he didn't disapprove. Colton wanted to own Eva, to know she'd always be his. He decided to put her before his fears, before the baggage from his past. Holding back wasn't saving Eva, only supplying him with an excuse to follow in his father's footsteps. But they were different men, and the only role model he'd ever needed was Mr. Ford.

"I want to be yours," she said. "I don't want to be alone."

Colton put his arm around her shoulders, holding her to his side. "That's good, because you should know by now how hard it is to get rid of us."

He watched the flames dance, the wood crackling as it slowly turned to ash. The stars were out, and the moon was full. These were the kind of nights he loved.

"It's back to the real world tomorrow," said North. "I don't even want to think about all the fields I need to plow."

"We'll get caught up," said Colton.

He wanted to bring up the topic of their ménage relationship because he was worried about the future, but Eva had enough on her plate. It was best not to stress her out anymore.

"The moon's big tonight," said Eva. "Remember the harvest moon last Halloween? I wonder if we'll get one again this year."

They'd stayed out in the corn fields all night. It had been an Indian summer, and the moon was huge and a brilliant orange. It appeared so close he swore he'd be able to touch it if he reached far enough. He remembered every detail of that night from the corn stalks poking him in the ribs to the sound of Eva's giggling. It seemed all his positive memories featured Eva Ford. Before her, before their dad walked out, his life was a haze of beatings, sadness, and chaos. Eva equaled happiness, safety, and laughter.

"I remember," said Colton simply.

North set his hand on her thigh. It meant nothing until Eva pushed his hand higher. She turned to look at his brother. "I can't forget last night," she said.

"Neither can I," said North.

"Are you going to keep pushing me away?"

His brother kept quiet.

"It's for your own good, Eva," said Colton. "You're not ready for more just yet."

"Why not? Because I'm twenty-two? Last time I

checked that's very much a woman." She sat straighter, not willing to lean on him any longer.

"But you're still our little Eva. All these changes are going to take time to get used to," he said. And it was true. One day he was her friend and protector, and the next they were declaring their romantic love for each other. It must have been there for a long time, growing and waiting for the perfect time to show itself.

"I don't need time to get used to you," she said. "Time is for people learning to trust. It's for people who aren't in love yet. Neither apply to me."

"So, what do you suggest, little one?" asked North. "You seem to know it all tonight."

"I want to be closer to both of you. There's only one way left to do that."

Colton swallowed hard. How could he refuse her? How could he agree? "You don't know what you're asking."

"You showed me last night." She turned to look him in the eyes. Even in the darkness, the moon picked up the blue notes in her eyes. "I want to go all the way, Colt. I want to feel your cock filling me."

He closed his eyes and took a deep, controlling breath before speaking. "You're a virgin, Eva. It'll hurt. I won't feel like you're thinking." It felt awkward talking about sex with Eva. She'd always been kept in a separate place in his mind, one far away from the darkness, including his one-nighters. Now she was his everything and he was terrified to make that transition.

"I don't care." She wrapped her little fingers around his open collar and leaned up to kiss him. Her tongue slid along the seam of his lips in a slow, sensual drag. "Touch me again."

They were out in the open but sheltered from the view of other trailers. He kissed her back, tasting her lips and losing himself to her innocent seduction.

She grabbed his hand and brought it to her crotch without breaking the kiss. He cupped her mound through her jeans making her gasp. "Yes, like that," she murmured.

North peppered kisses along the back of her neck, her body securely sandwiched between them as they sat on the old wooden bench by the fire.

"Are you sure this is what you want? We can still go back to the way things were," said Colton.

"This is exactly what I want."

He slid his hand up her sweater. Her skin was soft and warm against his calloused palm. He cupped her breast, using his thumb to roll her nipple.

"I love it when you touch me. North, touch me, too."

His brother didn't need to be asked twice. He wrapped an arm around her, finding his way to her other breast. She wriggled on the bench, rubbing her thighs together.

"You have the cutest little tits," said North. "I could suck them all night long."

"Do it."

Colton shook his head. "It's too cold out here for you, Eva. Let's get inside." He stood and helped her to her feet. North followed as they climbed the few step into the silver bullet. As soon as they were past the threshold, Eva threw herself against him, wrapping her arms around his neck. If she'd been any other woman, he'd have her on all fours by now. But this was Eva. His self-control would be put through a Herculean test tonight.

****

Eva felt like she was losing her mind. All she could focus on was muscles and sex. Every sight acted like an aphrodisiac—the scruff on Colt's jawline, the way North's jeans fit low on his hips, the plaid of their jackets, and the strength coiled in their forearms alone. Colton and North were sex on a stick, the kind of men who were every woman's type. Now that she saw them as much more than childhood friends, she was anxious to enjoy them, to explore their bodies in new intimate ways. Only they kept pushing her away, treating her like a child. Her confidence was taking a hit since she couldn't seem to give away her body even when trying.

But they were men. How long could they keep saying *no* to her?

Colt pushed her back as if her body scalded him. She turned to North instead. "Let me touch you." He'd refused her last night and she didn't want a repeat.

"Touch me all you want, sweetheart. I'm yours."

She immediately attempted to unbuckle the leather strap from his silver buckle. He stilled her hands.

"I want to touch what's mine," she said, determined.

He chuckled. "We have all the time in the world."

"You're both making me angry. Why do you keep refusing me?"

"Because you're too special," said Colt. "You're too special to have your first time in the loft of the silver bullet. You deserve a lot better than that."

She loved them so much. Meshing the unique love they'd always shared with this new intimacy was addicting. It added a whole new layer, creating so many things to discover.

"I only have good memories of this old trailer. I even remember when we used it as a fort until dad kicked us out." She ran the backs of her fingers along Colt's cheek. "This is my decision."

He cupped her face, holding a little harder than usual. His eyes were intense, a look a feral passion staring back at her. "Sex changes everything."

"It will never change how I feel about either of you." This time she dared to reach out and run her palm over the bulge in Colton's Wranglers. He bolted back as if she'd punched the air out of him. At least he couldn't hide his desire. No matter what sobering words he muttered, his rock-hard erection said otherwise.

Eva needed to show them just how committed she was to seeing this through. She'd lose her virginity tonight, even if it killed her. She pulled her sweater off over her head, letting it fall to the ground. She briefly massaged her own breasts before unzipping the front of her jeans.

"Holy shit, Eva. Behave yourself."

"Not tonight." She wriggled out of her pants until she was standing in just her white panties. She wished she had on something prettier, not the standard issue garments her mother bought her. Eva never thought about it before today.

The twins didn't say anything but they both raked their eyes up and down her body. She loved the heat of their stares on her intimate parts. Her body was thrumming with the need to be touched.

"North, are you hard for me again?" She could see his cock pressed diagonally across the front of his jeans. His size intimidated her but also roused her curiosity. She'd never seen a grown man naked.

He nodded.

Eva took a couple steps until she was able to press her body against his. "Take off your shirt," she said, fiddling with North's buttons.

North complied, pulling his partially tucked shirt out from his pants and tugged it off the top of his head. She was instantly hot. His skin was smooth and golden, ripped muscle after ripped muscle. Eva stood in front of him and ran both hands over his pecs, around his sides, and along his washboards abs. She never wanted to stop exploring, but out of nowhere, he grabbed her around the waist and hoisted her up on the kitchen counter a couple feet away. He forced his body between her legs, cupping her ass to slide her to the edge. She could feel his hard, denim-clad erection rubbing against her clit.

Her breathing turned to rapid pants as she hung onto his shoulders, waiting for him to act. His massive ribs expanded and contracted like an enraged bull. Maybe she'd been playing with fire all along.

She thrust her hips forward, loving the friction against her intimate parts. She was tired of waiting, of dreaming of the moment of penetration when her ache would finally be sated.

"Eva, you're not ready," said Colt, standing right beside his brother. They were the same height with the same broad cowboy shoulders. He leaned forward and sucked her breast slowly and thoroughly until her heartbeat was racing double time. "Your pussy's small and tight. I don't want us to hurt you."

"Don't make me beg," she said.

He growled in frustration, finally telling her to lean back on her elbows. She felt so exposed, but it thrilled her. Colt slipped off her panties, leaving her completely nude on the kitchenette counter. Thankfully, she trusted the McReed brothers with her life because she was acting completely out of character. They'd awakened something deep inside her, and she needed to trust them to teach her everything.

"What a pretty little pussy," said North. "So pink and ripe." He ran the tip of his finger along the moisture of her slit, up and down and all around her clit. Then he actually bent over and lapped his tongue up her folds. Eva screamed. It was such a dirty thing to do but exactly what she craved. The rush of electricity racing through her body took her by surprise.

"Yes, North! That feels so good."

"You taste fucking sweet, Eva." He spread her bent legs wide, Colton holding one knee open. North's hot breath stimulated her throbbing pussy before his tongue entered her. He was merciless, eating her like a starved man. She was teetering on a volatile edge, an orgasm threatening to break free at any second. Eva gasped for air, her arms flailing to the sides in search of anything to anchor her. A pot fell to the floor and cutlery scattered.

When North came up for a breath, Colt pushed him to the side, taking his place between her legs. He looked down at her swollen parts, only teasing with a feather-light touch. "If we're going to do this, I have to try and prepare you a bit," he said.

"Okay."

He showed her a bottle with "lubricant" written on the side. She watched as he drizzled some of the clear substance on two of his fingers. Just like last night he pressed those fingers into her pussy. Eva closed her eyes and focused on the fullness of the invasion. She clenched down on his fingers wishing they were his big cock instead.

"Relax for me, baby girl."

She hadn't realized her body was so tense, so she willed herself to melt around his fingers. Colt began to pump his two digits inside her. From her propped position on her elbows she could see everything he was doing. All three of them watched Colt finger-fuck her, occasionally scissoring his fingers to stretch her virgin hole.

"More," she chanted.

He smirked, pulling his fingers away, leaving her

wanting. Colton lubed up one finger this time, bringing it lower until he touched her asshole. She froze, unsure what he was going to do. When he slid that single finger up her ass, she gasped and nearly choked on all the wondrous new sensations flooding her bloodstream.

He kept his finger inside her forbidden hole as North leaned over to suckle her clit. Both men worked together, invading her with a menagerie of erotic experiences. She grabbed North's hair in a tight fist. An overload of powerful erotic pleasure assaulted her from numerous directions. Her ass was afire with need, her clit spasming under North's vigorous ministrations. She loved the untamed nature of the McReed twins. They were just as rough and raw in the bedroom as they were in every day left.

Colt used his big hand to easily cup her breast, his thumb teasing her nipple. It was the final push her body needed to leap over the edge. She cried out when her orgasm tore through her. North kept his lips on her clit while she rode out her release. She bucked on the counter as hands touched her everywhere. The rush of satisfaction took her to a new level of awareness. She was floating, soaring, all inhibitions washed away.

But if the brothers thought she'd stop begging for their cocks, they were in for a surprise.

Chapter Ten

North thought the zipper on his jeans would snap from the pressure. His cock was engorged and throbbing, his need to fuck making itself painfully clear. He'd spent the last ten minutes with his face buried between Eva Ford's legs. He never thought he'd see this day come. She was soft, sweet, and receptive. He could go down on her every day and it wouldn't be enough for him.

The scent of sex was strong in the trailer. Eva's eyes were glazed over, her lips swollen. She looked like an angel, her innocence slowly slipping away.

New powerful emotions surfaced inside him. Eva was his, and imagining any other man giving her the same pleasure seriously pissed him off. He wanted to protect her, love her, and for the first time, he wanted to conquer her.

"That's a good girl," said Colton, washing his hands off in the kitchen sink next to them. "Are you happy now that you've gotten what you wanted?"

His brother had more control than he did right now. It sounded like Colton wanted this party to stop before it started. North would follow his brother's lead because he couldn't trust his own judgement with Eva spread naked in front of him. As much as he wanted to stay away, he needed her more than ever.

Eva pushed herself up into a sitting position. "You know what I want," she said. "You told me you were preparing me for it."

He kissed her forehead. "Haven't you had enough for one night?"

She shook her head.

"What more do you want?" asked North. In truth, he wanted to hear her ask for it, to beg for his cock. He didn't think it was bad when nothing Eva did could lessen his love or respect for her. He was on a high. Sex had never been like this for him.

She focused on him, running her fingertips along the ridge of muscle on his shoulder. "I want to be as close as we possibly can," she said. "I want you inside of me."

"*Yes...*" North kissed her with all the passion burning inside him. He cupped her head with both hands. "I want to fill you with my cock, baby girl."

He pulled her off the counter until she wrapped her legs around him to keep from falling. As he carried her over to the loft, he continued to kiss her. Before he could climb all the way up, Colt's hand landed heavily on his shoulder.

"We can't undo this," he said.

"I don't want to." North was in this for the long haul. He was ready to devote the rest of his life to Eva, just as he'd given her the first part of his life.

He laid Eva on her back as he crawled over her. She immediately reached for his belt, and although his first reaction was to stop her, he let her continue. When she slid the zipper down, the pressure immediately began to ease. His cock was so thick and hard, it peeked out the top of his boxer briefs. Her exploring little fingers grazed the head of his cock, making his shudder.

Colton climbed up next to him. "You can't just fuck her, North. You'll hurt her."

He was ready to work her like a stud horse, but Colt was right, she was a virgin and needed a gentle introduction.

Eva wrapped her fist around his erection and the strength in his arms nearly gave out.

"She's holding my dick," he mumbled, hoping Colt would understand the urgency of the situation.

His brother passed him the tube of lube and a condom, giving him the unspoken permission to penetrate her first. It meant a lot to him for his twin to care that much. They both loved Eva in a way that rivalled the power of the sun. But they also loved each other more than any siblings could. North and Colton had been through so much together, and they'd survived.

"Relax, Eva. North's gonna give you what you want." Colton tossed his shirt and then settled down alongside Eva's body. She accepted him, seeking his lips for a kiss.

North rose to his knees and finished removing his buckle to release his cock. He fiddled with the condom wrapper. "Don't use that. I'm on the pill. I want the real you."

"Why you on the pill, Eva?" asked Colton.

"My mom got me on it when I was seventeen. It's to control my cycle."

"Even better," he said. "I've never had sex without one."

Eva watched him with wide eyes as he stroked the slippery lube along the length of his shaft. It was oddly erotic exposing himself in front of Eva. Part of him felt he was soiling her, but like she'd declared, she wasn't a little girl. She was very much a woman.

"Open your legs, darlin'."

She let her knees drop to the sides with no hesitation. His breath caught when he looked at her pussy in the dim lighting of the enclosed loft. The color reminded him of summer peaches, and he already knew how delicious she tasted.

"Slowly," reminded Colton.

"I know." He lowered over her, supporting his weight on one forearm.

North was practically shaking in anticipation. He

held the base of his cock and ran the head up and down, mingling the lube and her overflow of natural juices. Up close, his cock appeared too big to fit in her pale little pussy. Now he worried like Colton, afraid to hurt her.

When she began to writhe beneath him, staring at him with need in her eyes, he knew he couldn't wimp out now. He pressed the broad tip carefully between her pussy lips until he penetrated her. She gasped, but Colton whispered something in her ear, and she calmed.

"Change your mind yet?" He was surprised he was capable of speech at this point. Any longer and he'd come at the entrance of her hot little cunt.

"North stop playing," she said. "I need you." She reached both arms up for him, beckoning to lower himself completely over her prone body. He complied, holding the root of his erection as he dropped his weight over her. Every inch he lowered, the deeper his cock sank into Eva. She was so damned tight. Her virginity was speared by him, and the knowledge made him proud. His eyes lolled back in his head when he was finally fully seated.

Eva panted, in pleasure or pain he wasn't sure. He just kept reminding himself not to move, to allow her as long as she needed to adjust to his size. When she tested her inner muscles, he couldn't help but groan.

"Are you okay, Eva?" asked Colton. "Are you hurt?"

"I've never felt so full," she said. "He's big."

"That's because he's my twin."

North managed to punch his brother in the shoulder without moving his lower body. But he couldn't stay still forever. He'd been holding his breath, trying to think of things that turned him off. Even that was proving ineffectual. He pulled back, the lube aiding him in sliding out smoothly.

Eva reached out and held his shoulders. "Don't go," she gasped.

He smiled down at her. "We're just getting start, sweet thing." He thrust back in, slowly building a steady rhythm. His entire body broke out in a sheen of sweat as he kept his deepest desires bottled up tight.

Eva moaned, a guttural sound. "Oh God, that's so good."

He kissed her hard on the mouth. North was balls deep inside the only girl he'd ever loved. It was surreal. He began to fuck her harder, nipping her jawline, and sucking her pulse points. Any minute and he'd come, filling her with his essence, making them one.

****

Colton couldn't watch a minute longer. As soon as North reached his peak, he shoved his brother to the side. He'd already given him the gift of taking Eva's virginity. That was a prize above all others. But North had been dealt the short end of the stick in their family. He needed to give this to North to balance out some of the guilt he felt when their mother would strike out at him.

He'd already taken off his pants, and his cock had never been more ready. She was lost, grabbing behind his neck to bring his lips to hers. He kissed her, their tongues mingling as he sought her moist center. As they explored each other's mouths, he forced his dick into her hungry cunt. He easily slipped in, savoring the heat and tightness.

"You're mine now," he said. And he meant it. He'd never turn back now.

"I love you." Eva's nails dug into his shoulders, signalling she was close to another orgasm. His brother may have taken her first, but he'd get to feel her sweet little pussy milking his cock.

"Let it go, baby. Don't hold back."

He pumped his hips with enough stamina to go all night long. Each time he'd come down she'd make a sexy mewling sound that spurred him on.

"I'm almost there," she cried.

"Fucking come for me, Eva. Come," he demanded. "Come!" He punctuated each word by thrusting harder and faster. The entire silver bullet began to sway, the supports of the bed protesting.

"Colton! Colton!" Her body coiled tight, her muscles going rigid. She brought her arms and legs close as her inner walls clamped down on his erection. He choked out a sound between a cough and groan as she mercilessly squeezed him to completion.

When they were both limp with exhaustion, he rolled to his side of the bed, tucking her head into the crook of his arm. North flicked out the sheet, letting it settle over the three of them.

"You're full of our cum," said North, kissing the side of her neck. "I like that."

She was wedged between them, exhaustion nearly stealing her from consciousness. It was like so many other nights they'd share together. They found safety in each other. Now they'd taken things to a new level, a natural progression for their threesome.

"I can feel it on my thighs," she whispered.

"Do you want me to clean it off?" asked Colton.

She smiled. "No, I like it, too." Eva closed her eyes, her little hand resting on his chest. He loved that she trusted him, loved that she'd given them the gift of herself. He didn't deserve a good girl like her, but he'd spend the rest of his days showing her she hadn't made a mistake.

When the early rays of morning light filtered in the loft, he immediately ensured Eva was still between them. She looked like an angel, her blonde hair framing her face as she slept. He lightly touched her little pixie nose.

North stirred to life, narrowing his eyes from the light. His dark hair was disheveled and his stubble already growing in. He leaned up on one elbow. "We have to get the cows in the trailer and pack up," he spoke in a hushed tone. Eva was asleep between them. "Then we have to face the music."

"No shit," said Colton. "Not only do we have to deal with ma, we have to worry about how this will go over with Mr. and Mrs. Ford."

"There's no way it'll go over well. They'll fucking hate us. We'll wish we never crossed that line."

"I don't regret it," said Colton. "I just wished it was simpler."

North scoffed. "Since when have things ever been easy for us?"

They both looked down at the sleeping beauty. Later today they'd be back home in their old routines. Chester was a fantasy, so he worried how their new relationship would weather with a dose of harsh reality. He couldn't lose Eva.

Chapter Eleven

Colton unhitched the silver bullet and then took off in his pick-up with North. They'd been quiet on the way home, and she hated that uncomfortable feeling growing between them since she woke up in the morning. They hadn't even come to say hi to her mom and dad. She felt sad, like she'd ruined the best friendships she'd ever had because of her lust. Eva already missed them.

She dropped the gate of the trailer and walked Ruby out first. So many memories flooded her mind. It may have only been a week in Chester, but she'd lived more in that week than most of her life. So much happened. So much changed. By the time she emerged from the barn to get Bessie, her father was walking toward her from the house.

Eva just stood there, not moving to greet him or retreating. She was frozen with her emotions precariously under the surface. Her father's approval meant everything to her.

"Well, hello there, stranger."

"Hi, daddy."

"Any news for me?"

If only he knew the truth about everything. The biggest news was she'd slept with Colton *and* North, her childhood best friends. She'd lost her virginity and was no longer daddy's little girl. More than the sex was the revelation that they loved each other in ways far stronger than friendship.

"I wasn't first, but Bessie placed. We got a blue ribbon." She reached in her shirt pocket and pulled out her prize, waggling it out for him. When he reached her, he didn't take the ribbon, but rather pulled her into a tight hug. Her father's familiar rustic scent made her feel safe. She closed her eyes, a tear slipping out without warning.

"I missed you, Eva. I missed my sweet girl." He didn't let her go, as if the physical connection was all they had left. She didn't want things to change with her family, just as much as she knew things had to change if she wanted Colton and North in her life.

"Eva!" Her mother came running across the yard, a tea towel still in her hand. She stole Eva from her father, hugging and kissing her like she'd been gone a year not a week. "I'm so happy you're home. Where're the boys at? Dinner's almost ready."

"Gone home I guess."

"What's this?" Her mother noticed the blue ribbon in her hand. She took it, holding it up to the light to read. "You won a ribbon! My little Eva raised a prized cow all by herself."

She knew her mother would probably mount it amongst the family photos next to the fireplace. It was good to be home. Her parents were always loving and supportive, but just how deep did their support reach? Did they even realize she wasn't a child anymore?

After the reunion, she continued to offload her prize cow and settle her in the barn with Ruby. She took off her cowboy hat and ran a hand through her hair. The sun was close to setting, the clouds turning shades of red, orange, and pink. She began to think about the brothers again. Should she go over to offer a helping hand? They had a ton of work to get caught up since missing a week. She decided it would be best to stay away after her last unannounced visit ended disastrously. Eva hoped things were okay for them at home because she could never imagine the hell they were going through.

****

North slammed his truck door shut. "Why'd you

take off so fast? We didn't even get to see Mr. Ford."

Colton was already walking ahead, trying to avoid him. "I'm not going to be a two-face. I'll see him when there're no secrets between us."

"It would be better coming from us than Eva, don't you think?"

"Hell no. She'd kill us if we said a thing. You know how she is."

North caught up with his brother. There was a quiet, nervous tension between them because neither of them knew what to expect when they opened the door to their house. The lights were off inside despite the sun lowering on the horizon. It gave North an uneasy feeling. He immediately staked out the living room, noting some overturned furniture. The kitchen counter was full of dirty dishes and the fridge wasn't closed tight, creating a strip of light across the laminate.

"Ma?" he called out.

"I'll check her room," said Colton.

North did a quick sweep of the other rooms and bathroom, not finding their mother. Since they'd taken the keys and ensured she had no pills to abuse, it seemed impossible for her to get in any trouble. But when Colt screamed for him, he knew she must have found a way to support her habit.

"What's the matter?" he asked after bounding into her bedroom. She was passed out across her bed, several open pill bottles on her night side table. "Shit, how the hell did she get a hold of those?"

"She must have hidden them. Or someone brought them here."

"She breathing?"

"Her pulse is fine. She's just out cold," said Colton. "At least she's been eating and getting up."

North shook his head and stormed out of the

room. He crossed his arms and leaned against the wall in the hallway waiting for Colt. After his twin closed the door, he didn't hold back. "At least she's been eating? She did nothing but get high all week, Colt. I'm sick and tired of fucking babysitting her. She's not getting better and she doesn't want to. The only way she'll quit is when she stops breathing."

"She's still our mother."

"*How?* How is she our mother anymore? Does she do a lick of work around the house? Does she stay sober for more than a damn minute? Does she even give two shits about us?"

"I can't deal with this right now," said Colton, putting a hand to each side of his head. "We'll talk about this tomorrow."

He watched his twin walk down the hall to his room. North felt pumped up on adrenaline and ready to blow a gasket. He couldn't take any more of the same trials. There was only so much a man could take before he reached his breaking point.

He called out. "If she doesn't take Aunt Laura's offer soon, I'll fucking check her into rehab myself!"

North stopped to catch his breath. His first instinct was to rush over to Eva's house, to slip into her window and drown in her sweetness. He was addicted to forgetting his pain. But he'd ruined that refuge for himself by tainting Eva's innocence and building a wall between them and the Ford family. Until Eva explained their new relationship, it would be hard to face the family again. If their news wasn't accepted, he might never see Eva or the Fords again. That would be indigestible, just the thought making his stomach queasy.

He crashed onto his bed and stared up at the water-stained ceiling. What was Eva doing now? When he closed his eyes he could see the tin stars dangling from the ceiling, smell her sweet shampoo, and feel the plushness of her comforter.

Fuck, he felt trapped and lonely. These walls weren't a home, but a prison.

North rummaged in the top drawer of his night side table, pulling out a small stack of pictures. He sifted through them as he lay on his back. There were plenty of Eva throughout the years, some with the three of them, and one with just North and Eva sitting on a fence eating watermelon.

He had a couple of his father from before he left. There were many times he'd been tempted to burn them, and even Colton didn't know he kept them. He wasn't sure if he was holding onto them for the physical memory of the man or if he enjoyed torturing himself.

North rolled to his side when he flipped to a picture of his mother. She looked so happy. That was a long time ago. Her face wasn't gaunt, and her hair was brushed neatly off her face. He stared at it. Maybe if he looked long enough he could will his mother into the woman she once was.

He set the pictures back in the drawer. At this point, she'd end up killing herself if they didn't intervene. Colton thought he was doing their mother a favor by hiding the truth and covering up her frequent episodes. It only encouraged her self-destructive cycle. The answer was to call their Aunt Laura and ask her to help. She lived alone in Newcaster, a couple hours from them. It was a larger city with many resources and facilities made to help addicts. Living on the old ranch filled with memories of her love and loss only added to her sickness. Their mother needed a change of scenery, a fresh start in life before it was too late.

Just as North realized the same applied to him.

****

Eva went over her list one last time. Her father wanted definitive numbers for the big corn roast coming up in a week. This would be the biggest yet. Although she'd been overly excited about the event before leaving for Chester, it was difficult to inspire herself now. It had been a week since they'd come home, and she hadn't seen Colton or North once. Each day felt like a lifetime, her zest for life slowly slipping away. Part of her wondered if they wanted to write her off, but in her heart she knew they were waiting on her. She was expected to announce their relationship to her old-fashioned parents. It chilled her to the bone just thinking about it. Every day she'd promise herself she'd do it tomorrow, but tomorrow never came.

Eva found her dad in the barn, unsaddling his riding gelding. Dust motes danced in the rays of light peeking in through the knots in the wood. It smelled familiar of hay and manure.

"I have the list," she said.

He turned to her, staring for a few long moments before beckoning her closer with a crooked finger. "Something you're not telling me?"

She shook her head. "Why would you ask?"

"Well, for one, it's the first week the McReed twins haven't offered to help with the cattle or show up for a meal. Seems odd to me."

Her nerves flared. "I'm sure they're just busy getting all caught up."

He tilted his head as he studied her. She felt like glass—fragile and transparent. He hated it when she lied. Most of her punishments had been for lying, and her heart beat double time under his suspicious glare.

"But they'll be at the corn roast, no?"

"Of course. I mean, I don't see why not."

He lifted up her chin. "You haven't been yourself

since coming back from Chester, Eva. You look…sad. I don't like it.

She wanted to offer him part of the truth because she needed his love and acceptance, now more than ever. "I went to the city for a lot more than a ribbon. I wanted to show you I was capable, to show you I'm not just a child anymore."

Her father smiled. He always had a sense about people, able to look past the exterior to the goodness within. It was one of the reasons she loved him so much.

"You'll always be *my* child, Eva." He pulled her into a tight embrace as he petted her hair. "But I'm also proud of the young woman you've become. I never doubted you, never saw you as incapable. I'm just a foolish daddy worried too much about his baby girl."

"You're not foolish," she cried. Her tears soaked his plaid shirt. They came seemingly out of nowhere. She'd been a basket case since coming home because she knew what had to be done.

"I need to remember you're nearly twenty-three, not ten. It won't be long until you're ready to start your own family, and I'll be beside you every step of the way. Next time I mess up, you make sure to give me a swift kick." He cupped her face and kissed each of her closed eyelids moist from tears. "No more crying now. We have a corn roast to plan, and I'm going to do something a little extra special for you this year."

She smiled up at him. "Thank you, daddy."

Eva started to return to the house but decided she couldn't sit idle any longer. She needed to know what Colton and North were thinking. God, she needed to see them. It was torturous being separated for so long. She didn't even realize how engrained they were in her life until they were no longer in it.

She mounted her Palomino mare and rode across

the fields to the McReed farm. Their little bungalow came into view, but the tractor in the distance caught her eye next. She steered her horse to the left and galloped across the partially plowed barley fields. The twins kept her father's cattle in hay for most of the winter.

When she neared, she knew it was Colton in the tractor. The sunlight made the blond highlights in his hair appear like rays of gold. She rode a wide circle around his tractor to signal him to cut the engine. Growing up on a working farm, she knew better than to risk life and limb around the deadly blades of farming equipment.

The rumble of the tractor wound down until silence returned to the morning. She dismounted her horse and rushed over to see Colton. Her spirits lifted just being near him, but he didn't greet her like he usually did. Colton didn't get off his seat and his face remained stoic.

She swallowed hard, not even attempting to climb up into the cab like she usually did. "Hi," she said. "I've missed you."

He looked straight ahead, not even turning to acknowledge her. "You tell your dad about us yet?"

"Not yet," she said. Eva knew she'd been stalling all week. It wasn't an easy thing to do. She had to tell her parents that she planned to spend the rest of her life with not one, but two men. It was unheard of but also the only answer for her. "I was thinking maybe after the corn roast."

"Sure, Eva." Then he turned to face her, his emotions guarded. "I don't think you ever plan on telling him."

"It's not exactly simple. Have you told your mother?"

"Our mother's gone. She left two days ago."

Eva felt like a monster for having mentioned

Karen McReed in the first place when it was only to take the focus off herself. "What do you mean, Colt?"

"I mean she's fucking gone. It's the story of my life, didn't you know that? People leave. I'm over it." He started up the tractor again, the sudden noise spooking her horse. "And I expect no less from you, baby girl."

She watched him drive away.

Eva felt numb. Part of her wanted to chase after Colton. She wanted to apologize, to tell him she was different than all the people who'd hurt him. That she loved him. This was the first time he'd ever raised his voice at her. He'd always been kind and patient, and never brushed her off. Maybe she'd pushed the brothers away for good.

When she turned around, she could only see the distant image of her horse as it headed back home without her. Eva had a long walk ahead of her.

Chapter Twelve

North stood on the front porch, staring out into the darkness. Colt hadn't come home. Yesterday, after working the land, he'd taken off to town. He came home plastered, not willing to talk about anything. Tonight, he didn't come back at all.

He was worried sick about his twin. Ever since their Aunt Laura came to pick up their mother a few days back, Colt had changed. It was like he hated the world for shitting on him and North even more for making that phone call. What choice did he have? Colton didn't realize all the sacrifices he'd made for their mother during his life. He loved her, but he couldn't sit idly by another day while she wasted away.

Now the house was empty—void of both hate and love. It was a place. Four walls. North wanted more. He wanted his brother back. He wanted Eva.

He returned to the warmth of the house, the screen slapping back into place as he shut the main door. He had a good fire going, the flames glowing brightly behind the glass of the wood stove. The rest of the house was quiet, dark, and empty. North squatted down, mesmerized by the strength of the fire. The mix of colors in the flames danced and intermingled, beautiful yet deadly.

What was happening to him? He didn't even have anger left. North felt lost, deflated, lacking any motivation beyond surviving another day.

The best thing he could do was get some sleep. He'd probably have to take care of Colt's share of work come morning, so he'd need his energy. North walked down the hall to his room, stopping at his mother's door by habit. It felt foreign not to worry about her anymore.

She was in good hands, getting the help she needed. Despite what Colt thought, North knew he'd saved her. She'd been given a ticket out of the McReed house. How many times had he prayed for one himself?

He pulled off his T-shirt and kicked off his Wranglers after entering his room. The light from the moon reflected off his mirror, giving him enough light to sort out his quilts before crashing into bed. The old springs protested from his weight. He closed his eyes, taking deep cleansing breaths. He kept telling himself that tomorrow was another day, and things could only get better. Although Eva had been a forbidden topic between him and Colton, equal to a deadly sin, it didn't stop him from thinking about her. He tried to remember the exact shade of her hair, the smell of her shampoo, and the sound of her laughter.

Each day he hoped she'd prove Colton wrong by telling Mr. Ford what had started between the three of them. If things went bad, he'd never turn his back on her. But he was beginning to wonder if she regretted everything they'd shared. Should he have worked harder to resist her? Refused her altogether?

He must have finally dozed off because the sound of the window rattling behind his bed startled him back to consciousness. He leapt to his feet just as the glass was lifted partway up. North was ready for a fight, all his muscles tense.

"North, help me."

It was Eva, attempting to heave herself through the small opening. Rather than turning on the light, he lifted the old stubborn windowpane all the way up and helped her inside. She crawled onto his bed, finally settling on her knees.

"What in God's name are you doing here? Do you realize what time it is?"

"Late," she whispered. "But I had to see you."

"Why?" This was the first time she'd ever come to their house. She didn't belong in their world, and maybe it was wishful thinking to believe they could ever belong in hers. North's first reaction was to force her to leave. But his mother was gone, and there was nothing he wanted more than Eva.

"I've messed everything up. Colton won't even talk to me. I don't know what to do."

"He's just hurting."

She beckoned him closer with outstretched arms. "I've missed you."

He stood tall at the side of his bed, afraid to let down his guards. How the fuck was he supposed to feel at this point?

"Did you come here to play games, Eva?"

"Stop it, please. I'm not trying to be the bad guy, North. I'm just scared." She started to cry, so softly it was barely audible.

"Mr. Ford is a reasonable man."

"I'm going to tell him. I have no choice."

"Why not?"

"Because I can't lose you."

This time he stepped into her reach at the edge of the bed. She hugged him around the waist, resting her head on his bare chest. "All I think about is you," he admitted.

She shifted her head and kissed his chest. One kiss led to several. Eva ran her hands up his back, trying to pull him down once she reached his shoulders.

He shook his head. "No, Eva. Not here. Not like this."

"Kiss me."

How could he not be affected by her? He'd been dreaming about her every night, replaying their nights of passion over and over in his head. North leaned down and kissed her, not expecting it to carry such an emotional punch. He was immediately lost, as if the taste of her lips held his undoing.

"God, I've missed you," he murmured against her lips North leaned forward until she was forced to her back and beneath him. All the pain, fear, loneliness, and everything in between was released in a massive rush of energy. He stripped off her shirt, kissing every inch within reach. "I fucking need you." His cock was instantly ready, his entire body reacting to Eva's presence. Everything happened so fast. They couldn't touch each other enough, as if they'd both die without contact.

"Make love to me."

She didn't need to ask him twice. There was nothing he wanted more. North slid his hand down the front of her jeans as he kissed her so deep he wasn't sure where each of them started.

"You're wet for me," he said. Her pussy was hot and swollen, his finger easily slipping inside. Less than two weeks ago she'd been a virgin, now she was his.

"*Yes.*" She helped him unbutton and remove her jeans, along with her panties. They both rushed, sexual desperation taking control. "I need you inside me, North. I can't even sleep at night thinking of you."

The yearning in her voice made it difficult to think with a level head. He thrust himself between her legs, sliding the entire length of his cock into her tight little cunt. She wrapped her legs securely around him, crying out once he filled her to the hilt.

"I love your pussy, Eva." He wanted to say it belonged to him. That *she* belonged to him, but he bit his tongue instead. "I want to fuck you all day, every day."

He suckled the erogenous zone behind her ear as

he began to work her body. She was so receptive, writhing to meet him thrust for thrust. Her satisfied moans encouraged him to take her harder and faster. His headboard crashed against the wall with each pump his hips.

He stopped to catch his breath. Sex with Eva was as close to heaven he thought he'd ever get.

****

Eva wanted to ask for Colton, craving the dual stimulation along with Colt's acceptance. Instead, she focused on North's massive frame hulking over her, his cock pumping deliciously in and out of her pussy. His erection was so thick and swollen there wasn't a cell inside her not being stimulated at once. It felt amazing to connect with one of the McReed twins after mourning their loss for over a week. Being with North only confirmed the fact she had to solidify their ménage à trois as soon as possible.

Living without them wasn't an option.

"I love you," she whispered in his ear. Eva needed him to know it. She hated that the twins thought she was brushing them to the side with disregard. It was anything but the truth.

"You're mine," he grated, the sound a mix of raw masculinity and possessiveness. North worked her body with stamina, never faltering. He reminded her of an animal, feral and hungry. They were a mass of limbs, clean sweat, and sex.

She held onto his biceps as he supported his weight over her body. His muscles were rock-hard and massive, his skin warm. Knowing how capable he was turned her on even more. She could feel an orgasm mounting each time his pubic bone brushed her clit. He was like a beast, fucking her like he'd been holding back for years.

"Come for me, Eva."

Those words were like magic. She wasn't sure if it was the dominance in his tone or the fact he'd asked it of her at all, but the orgasm came rushing to the surface like a freight train. It exploded from her womb, sending a cascade of perfect peace to every extremity. Her pussy walls clamped down on North's cock, pulsing on and on.

Before her body went limp from exhaustion, North growled as he filled her with his hot cum. The scruff on his cheek scraped her as he nuzzled her neck. Even his scent was familiar. She held him tight to her, loving how sex brought them closer.

"I don't want to leave," she said, her breathing still labored. "I want to stay here just like this." Eva didn't want him to even remove his semi-flaccid cock.

He kissed the corner of her mouth. "Your parents will worry."

"I snuck out my window," she said. "They'll never know."

He exhaled, dropping and rolling to his back so she could rest over him. "You're a woman now, Eva. You don't have to sneak around like a teenager. You can make your own choices."

"I'm going to tell him right after the corn roast. I promise." She painted patterns on his shoulder with a fingertip. "You're coming, right?"

"I'm coming."

"And Colt?"

"He's a bit of a mess right now," said North. "He's been drowning his sorrows in cheap whiskey."

"He has to come. He always does."

"Things aren't exactly the same anymore, darlin'. We've gone and complicated our lives. All of us." He ran his hand through her hair. She could hear his strong heartbeat beneath her ear. It was familiar and soothing.

"But I still don't regret a thing."

As peaceful as she felt in North's arms, she worried about Colton. It was the middle of the night and he was off drinking and doing God knows what. Would he have one of his usual sexual flings? She remembered how much the cowgirls in town flocked to the McReed brothers. It never mattered to her before, but it did now. The thought made Eva feel territorial and jealous. Even though she hadn't held up her end of the bargain by telling her father about their relationship, she hoped Colton would have waited for her. Did his love have an expiry date?

"Maybe he's moved on. Just because you're twins doesn't mean he feels the same way about me as you."

"I know my brother," said North. "He cares about you just as much as I do."

"I saw him yesterday. He couldn't stand the sight of me."

He stroked her hair. "Our father wasn't a good man, Eva. Colt's afraid he's destined to fill his boots. He's rethinking everything."

She pushed up on her forearms. "What do you mean?" Panic lashed about inside her like a dragon's tail.

He cooed for her to calm. "He misses the way things used to be, and he doesn't want your daddy disappointed with him. We both owe him a lot."

"I won't let him walk away from me. You have to talk to him, North."

"Sleep, Eva. Everything's better in the morning."

****

Colton staggered to the bench across the street from the pub. He'd pushed his limit, and his stomach already protested. But how else was he supposed to handle the pain? Everything was happening at once, the shitload of stress growing to intolerable levels.

His mother was gone, probably for good, carted across the state to Newcaster. He wanted her home, well, and independent like she had been once upon a time. He wanted to recapture the fantasy of his mother when she was young and full of optimism. It was bad enough that his father walked out on the family, now his mother had done the same, even if not by choice. She'd chosen her addiction. And Eva had chosen her perfect life over a loser like him.

Just thinking about Eva made his heart race. She held the key to his heart, yet she tossed it with disregard. He'd loved her every day of his life, and he never refused her anything. Even when she wanted to change their relationship to something new and intimate, he'd tried to pull away to preserve what they had. Now everything was fucked.

She bided her time like a black widow, waiting until he fell so fucking hard in love before she struck. Of all the people and shit in his life, he never expected to be destroyed by little Eva Ford. She'd always been his saving grace, the light in the darkness. Did he still want her? More than breath. But as much as she harped about wanting to start a family of her own, she wasn't moving very fast introducing them as her men.

He stumbled along the sidewalk, deciding there was nothing better to do than head home. He was confronted by one of the Irish cowboys from the large hog farm just east of town. Colton and North had been friends with the three brothers since grade school.

"Colton, you looking for trouble?"

It was pitch black out, only the odd streetlight highlighting the road. "Don't fuck with me now, Donal. I'm not in the mood."

"Look at him, Liam, he's angrier than feral hog."

Colton was drunk, heartbroken, and depressed. Things couldn't get much worse. The two brothers flanked him as they walked up the abandoned road. Crickets droned in the tall grass in the neighboring fields.

Liam tilted his Stetson, giving him the once over. "He looks lovesick, he does. Maybe he's thinking of that Ford girl in unholy ways." He was nearly as loaded as Colton, but he was also a big guy who could hold his liquor.

"You need to watch your damned mouth," said Colton, trying his best to ignore the brothers. His logic and self-control were at the bottom of a bottle, and it wouldn't take much more to set him off, especially when they mentioned Eva.

The headlights of a pickup truck highlighted cones on the road ahead as it passed him, the loud twang of country music filling the night air. It slowed to a stop just ahead, and Connor leaned out the driver's side window. "Hurry up, the two of you, or I'll make you walk home."

"We're coming," called Donal. "Give our friend a ride, too. He looks like shit."

Colton wasn't thinking straight, flashbacks of his father flashing in his head. The alcohol was supposed to kill the memories, not aggravate them. When Liam set a hand on his shoulder, Colton threw a punch, landing him square on the jaw. He didn't expect his aim to be so sure when he could hardly walk straight. He supposed he did have a death wish. He'd just struck one of the O'Brian brothers while the other two watched. Colton knew the love between siblings well. He was ready for a shit storm of trouble, and part of him craved it. What did he have to lose?

"Did he just clock you?" asked Donal. "And you just stood there like a doorstop?" He laughed out loud, and Connor did the same.

"I'd hate to piss you off when you're sober." Liam chuckled and wrapped a heavy arm around him, leading Colton to the bed of the truck. "You know I was just teasing about Eva, Colt."

Both brothers heaved him into the back of the truck like an oversized bag of feed, climbing in next to him. They both wore heavy quilted jackets like Colton's. The breeze was bitterly cold at this hour.

They dropped him off in front of his ranch. He had nothing to go home for, but he trudged down the path regardless.

"We'll see you at the corn roast, McReed," Connor called out before hitting the gas. He jumped back to avoid the spray of gravel.

The wash of moonlight aided him in finding his way to the barn. He climbed the rickety ladder to the hay loft and crashed down on a bed of flakes. There was no way he wanted to get into a heated battle with North at this hour—not when he was exhausted, pissed off, and nauseated. He still remembered the last time he saw Eva out in the fields. It took all his resolve not to break down and beg her to love him. But he knew too well that he couldn't inspire love in another.

Chapter Thirteen

"Come on, what are you waiting for?"

North had waited on the porch for five minutes while Colton stalled inside. The Fords expected them to come by first thing in the morning to shuck for the corn roast, and it was already ten o'clock.

"This ain't a good idea," said Colton. "It feels wrong."

"We help them with the corn roast every year. It'll be more weird for us not to show up."

"*She'll* be there."

"And?"

"And I'm not ready to talk to her just yet." Colton grabbed the truck keys and walked ahead of him.

"She promised to talk to her dad after the roast. I believe her."

"I don't believe in anyone—no disappointments that way." Colton boarded the truck and slammed the door shut. North joined him in the cab.

"You're going to upset her, Colt. You need to get a fucking grip."

North hadn't told his brother about his night with Eva, not when he was hurting so much. He was quickly slipping into his old ways—drinking, fighting, pissing off the world. Still, he couldn't keep pushing her away. She was still their Eva, still special, even if nothing developed from their brief romance.

"You don't understand," he said. "She's corrupted me."

North laughed as they drove up the back road towards the Ford house. "I don't think that's possible. Do you really believe the shit coming out of your mouth?"

"I can't even look at another woman without

thinking of her. I can't eat. I can't sleep. I can't even jerk off for God's sake."

"It's called love, Colt. I feel the same thing. It won't kill you."

Colton shook his head. "It already is. I feel like shit without her."

As they pulled onto the Ford property, there were already people gathering around the area. Large drums of corn were waiting for their attention. He scanned the area for Eva, but he couldn't spot her.

"It won't be long until everything's settled," North assured.

His twin didn't even respond, exiting the truck with an air of nonchalance. He was a pro at putting on his game face, but North supposed he was no different. It was easier to pretend they were happy than needing to explain why they weren't.

Mrs. Ford spotted them first. She rushed over and wrapped an arm around Colton's waist. "Where have you two been hiding?"

"Just busy," said North, when Colton didn't reply.

"Well, stop being strangers. It doesn't feel natural with the two of you not underfoot. And too much food is going to waste."

"Yes, ma'am," he said.

Colton looked pale. He knew his brother was worried about disappointing Mr. and Mrs. Ford. No matter how hard he tried to replicate disinterest, he couldn't hide his real feelings from North.

"You ready to shuck?" She smiled up at both of them. He had a feeling she knew something was up, but she didn't push for more information. Today was supposed to be a fun day.

They found two wooden stools and got straight to

work. There was a mountain of corn to prepare. Colton kept quiet. North just wanted the day to be over with.

Over an hour passed, and they managed not to speak to each other. North was lost in thought most of the time.

"Howdy, strangers." Mr. Ford approached them from the barn. He coiled a length of rope around his hand and elbow.

"Afternoon," said North.

He paced the area, watching them shuck, not talking. North swallowed hard, wondering if Eva had said anything yet. There was an unspoken tension in the air.

"There're a lot of people coming," he finally said. "It seems Eva's invited half the town...including the Blackwood sisters." He chuckled, swinging the coiled rope over his shoulder.

Neither of them said a word.

"You're both quiet. Something you want to tell me, Colton?"

Shit. Mr. Ford was like a lion, sensing weakness in his brother. Would Colt break under the pressure?

"No, sir," said Colton.

"Eva's been quiet, too. Either of you know anything about that?"

Mr. Ford was suspicious. He always did tend to sense their moods or when something was amiss. He was about to give Mr. Ford an excuse, something to take the heat off them and Eva until she decided to tell him herself.

But Colton decided to speak up. "A lot happened on the trip. We started—"

He elbowed his brother hard in the side. "Look, there she is!"

Colton would ruin everything, no doubt putting

his foot in his mouth and making the situation harder than it needed to be. Eva approached them, hooking her arm around her father's arm.

"Thanks for coming," she said.

"Our pleasure." North stared up at her from his stool. She'd fancied herself up for the corn roast, her long blonde loose down her back rather than in a pigtail. It was odd watching her from afar. Normally she'd run into his arms with a smile. He didn't like the distance growing between them.

A truck honked several times. Three pickup trucks pulled in.

"We'll talk later," said Mr. Ford. "It looks like your surprise is here, Eva."

They walked away, Eva looking back once. He couldn't look away. She was so beautiful.

He turned to Colton. "Next time keep your big mouth shut," said North. "Eva needs to tell him herself."

"Well, I ain't going to lie to him. He's more than a father to me, and I won't ruin that trust."

"You'll ruin a lot more than that if you don't keep quiet."

He peeled the corn, tossing the ready ones in an oversized cooking pot. The entire time he kept his focus on Mr. Ford and Eva greeting their guests. The cars and trucks flooded in now, a new one parking every few minutes.

"I'm skipping out when we're done," said Colton.

"You think the Fords won't notice?"

That's when he saw Luke Weston and his family chatting them up. Mr. Ford seemed overly enthusiastic, even putting his arm around Luke and motioning Eva to come closer.

"What's going on over there," Colt asked, finally showing interest. He dropped a corn into the pot with a thud and stood up to get a better look.

"Can't know for sure."

Luke Weston was twenty-three and the heir to a thriving cattle operation just outside of town. He was what they called a pretty-boy, sitting back while hired hands did all the dirty work.

When Eva and Luke strolled off alone together, North's hackles went up. They never let men near Eva, and it felt immeasurable worse doing nothing now that his feelings for her had changed. He wanted to toss the shucking job and ask Luke what the fuck his problem was.

The two disappeared in the growing crowd. His chest tightened around his heart. As soon as they were out of sight, Colt leapt to his feet and rushed after them.

"Colt, wait!" He followed his brother. "You can't do anything."

"Watch me."

At least his twin wasn't lying to himself anymore. He wanted Eva and denying it didn't change the fact. When they reached the edge of the white brick house, Mr. Ford blocked their way.

"Where you going, boys?"

Colton's quiet brooding was apparently over. He tried to look past Mr. Ford. "I saw Luke leading Eva this way."

"I know you're used to protecting her, and that's good, but she's getting older now. She wants to grow up in hurry, find a husband, and start her own life. The least I could do was steer her in the right direction. You have nothing to worry about where Luke is concerned."

Holy shit, Mr. Ford was setting Eva up with that counterfeit cowboy. And they couldn't do anything about it without telling him they were both hot and bothered for his only daughter.

"You sure that's what Eva wants?" asked Colton.

"She told me she wanted to go to Chester to prove she was an independent woman. She wants the freedom to plan her own future," said Mr. Ford. "I suppose she's ready to know what love's all about."

"Why Luke?"

"He's a good boy from a good family. I couldn't ask for anything more."

"Right." Colton rocked on his feet. "I mean, I'm sure he's great. Eva deserves the best."

"Just give her some space. I'm sure she'll be better for it."

"Sure. Yeah. No problem."

A swarm of family and friends gave them the chance to slip away. Colton walked so fast that North could barely keep up.

"Wait up," called North.

Colt whirled around once they were alone near the barn. "Can you believe this shit?" He paced in a circle, his anger and frustration palpable. "He's from a *good family*. Did you hear him, North? And what are we, worthless castoffs?" He punched a hand into his fist.

"That's not what he meant. He doesn't even have a clue we love Eva."

"Don't matter. That's his reasoning, so we have no hope of making this work. Maybe he's right. No, I know damn well he's right, which is why I pushed her away to start with."

"Lower your voice, Mrs. Ford's coming this way."

Eva's mother came straight for them, a smile on her face. She handed them each a shortbread biscuit. He missed her home cooking. "It's time to gather 'round the bonfire," she said.

North narrowed his eyes. "What bonfire?"

She put her hands on her hips, and he finally caught on. They had always been the ones to shuck the corn, set up the bonfire, and help keep the day running smoothly. His mind was elsewhere. In fact, Colt's idea of skipping out was a tempting prospect with his emotions on his sleeve.

****

After getting the bonfire roaring, Colton stepped back to admire his handiwork. They had a few hours of daylight left, but the fire would stave off the chill and it was a focal point for the guests of the corn roast. Children ran by, forcing him to arch his back to keep out of their way. He should be happy, and the event usually put him in good spirits, but he needed more than corn, booze, and friends. Colt needed Eva.

North had grabbed a table for them on the periphery. There were a lot of families and groups of cowboys waiting for Mr. Ford to give his annual speech. He'd give thanks to God for the harvest, his family, and friends. He'd make his predictions for next spring's weather, and he'd tell funny stories involving locals everyone knew well. He'd surely mention Eva and Bessie's blue ribbon. Maybe he'd throw in something about Eva tying the knot with Luke Weston. He ground his teeth together just imagining her with another man.

Colton wanted to be the one Mr. Ford spoke about with pride. He wanted to be good enough for Eva. But those were fantasies, not unlike the ones he had as a boy when he wished for someone to save him from the hell at home. Nobody ever came.

Once the speeches were through, everyone began to talk, eat, and socialize. The music was pumped through the portable speakers bringing a sense of carefree abandon to the event. Colton sat back and watched all the partygoers, his eyes continually roving about for Eva or Luke. He'd grabbed a couple beers from the cooler, and he wondered how many he'd have to drink to ease the pain. The pain of watching Eva fall in love with the man her father chose for her.

"Look who's coming," said North, nudging him in the ribs.

It was Lorna and Katie Blackwood. The sight should have made his cock hard. They wore short shorts despite the cool temperature, but they were known around town for their flirtatiousness. Colton used to play along, and normally he wouldn't be against fucking either of them behind the barn.

Now he wasn't so sure.

"Why are you two sitting over here all by yourselves?" asked Lorna. She fluffed up her hair and sat next to him.

"Just taking a breather."

"You don't mind if we keep you company?" asked Katie.

"Suit yourself," said Colton. This was what Mr. Ford expected of him. He was only good for one thing, making a complete ass of himself. Why didn't Eva's father think of *him* when setting her up? Why was he only good enough for the town tramps?

"I heard you went to Chester," said Lorna. "I've always wanted to go there. How was it?"

Colton eyed the bonfire, the shadow of Eva appearing behind the flames. He stood up to get a better look. "North…"

His brother joined him, standing and looking off into the distance.

"Colton?" Lorna's voice grated on his nerves.

"We should get a closer look," said North.

He mentally scolded himself. "No, this is her choice, like Mr. Ford said. I ain't going to force myself on her."

"Who are you looking at?" asked Katie.

He turned to the women, trying to keep his manners while wishing they were gone. "Nobody."

When Eva began to walk in their direction, he scrambled to get in his seat and appear nonchalant. He didn't want her to know how much he was pining over her.

She looked so fucking pretty, her blonde hair fluttering softly behind her. He wanted to hold her, kiss her, and drown in her sweetness. God, he missed her.

"Hi," she said. Where had her smile gone? Was he the one to chase it away? Eva stood in front of their table; her face solemn. Just hearing her voice settled something inside of him. She was the key to his sanity. "Can I talk to both of you for a minute?"

"Where's Luke?" He couldn't help himself. His jealously had been brewing since he first saw her walk off with the other man.

She frowned. "What do you mean?"

He leaned over his knees, his beer bottle dangling from one hand. Lorna's hand travelled up and down his back, and Eva watched the motion. "I mean Luke Weston, the great guy with your daddy's blessing."

"That's not fair," she said. "Can I please talk to you in private?"

The sky had dimmed a degree and the sunset wouldn't be far off with the shorter autumn days. Country music hummed in the air, enhancing his volatile emotions. Why couldn't he catch a break? Did God hate him that much? It seemed like he'd been treading water his entire life, never able to reach his goals.

North rose to his feet.

"Fine," he said, standing next to his brother. Before walking away, he turned to the Blackwood sisters and tipped his Stetson in farewell.

They followed Eva through the bustling yard, weaving in and out of groups of people. Colton knew most of them, and not one turned a head as the three of them passed. They'd been a trio for over a decade, and the Ford house was their second home. Only he couldn't go back to seeing Eva as the little girl next door—no matter how hard he wanted to.

When they turned the corner around the large livestock barn, Eva shoved him against the wooden wall boards. Her eyes were red-rimmed and her breathing heavy.

"Why are you doing this to me?" She pressed her hands to his chest to keep him in place. "You have no right!"

"You think you can overpower me?"

"Whatever, Colt. I just want you to talk to me. You're acting like a stranger."

He stared at her for a long moment. "Maybe it's better that way."

Tears slipped down her cheek and she choked on her words. "You're supposed to love me!"

Colton took a deep breath. How could he keep feigning disinterest when she looked up at him with such vulnerability in her eyes? He was hardwired to look out for her and keep her happy. All he'd done since coming home was make a mess of everything.

"I've been waiting for you to tell your dad about us, but you keep putting it off. Now I guess I know why," said Colton.

"Are you suggesting I have a have a flame burning for Luke?" She'd raised her voice, the hurt in her tone making him feel like a jackass. "I don't care how much money he has or how perfect his family is, because that's what you're thinking, Colton McReed. I know you too well."

"Your daddy sure approves."

"I don't want Luke!"

"Well you've got me at a loss then, Eva. What is it you want?"

She fiddled with the buttons on his shirt. Her hair fell to the sides of her face when she looked down. "Do you really have to ask?"

Chapter Fourteen

The annual corn roast carried on long into the night. By the time things started wrapping up the moon was out, and the brisk wind had the partygoers pulling on sweaters and blankets. Although it had been an exciting day overall, it wasn't the same as other years. Eva could feel the tension between her the twins like winter molasses.

Eva took Colt and North by the hand and led them away from the festivities. Her father had some crazy idea that she needed help planning out her own life. She knew he meant well, but he couldn't inspire her to love Luke Weston. Her whole heart belonged to the McReed brothers, and he'd have to accept that once she told him.

She needed to get them alone, away from her father and all other prying eyes. She craved intimacy, that unique connection they shared in Chester.

"Where we going?" asked North. They walked through the tall grass to the back of the house and then down the slope to the old hay barn. It was pitch black when they turned the corner, the distant flood lights at the front of the property blocked out.

"It's a secret."

When they got to the barn, she climbed up the wooden ladder to the loft. She used to play up here when she was a kid, so it brought back fond memories when she saw nothing had changed. Eva used the quilt she'd been holding around her shoulders and set in on the ground in her favorite spot. She settled on her back and looked up through the exposed roof boards. In all these years, her father hadn't repaired the damage caused from the big ice storm that pummelled their outbuildings. She was glad for it.

"You can see the stars," she said. Once her eyes adjusted to the dim surroundings, the moon and stars gave the loft a wash of light.

Colt squatted next to her, looking at her like she was a puzzle to solve.

She pointed up. "Look, it's the big dipper."

When she turned her head to the side, Colton was staring at her rather than the sky. "I can't do this, Eva. I'm sorry, baby girl, I've fucked up everything."

His shaggy blond hair fell down over his eyes as he settled next to her. He was stunning, the moonlight highlighting the masculine planes of his face. She knew he was hurting, and not just because of her. All she wanted to do was make everything right.

She touched his face, wishing he'd kiss her. "I want to belong to both of you. In every way." Eva had been obsessing over the brothers during the long, lonely nights at home. She kept wishing they'd knock on her window, but they never came. "I've been dreaming about our night in Chester."

Colton's jaw clenched.

"What if your father doesn't approve after you tell him?" asked North. "Will you forget about us then?" He was still standing up, leaning against a support beam. His dark features blended with the shadows, but the faint lighting reflected off the metal of his belt buckle.

"I'm a grown woman. If he doesn't accept the men I love, then he doesn't accept *me*."

North walked around the barren loft, each step punctuated with a hollow echo and occasional creek in the wood. "That would be a big sacrifice. Maybe too big."

"Some things are worth fighting for," she said.

The McReed brothers had literally been fighting for her all their lives. They protected her, coddled her, and made her feel safe in every way. How could she walk away from them now that her love burned hotter than the sun?

North peeked in the burlap sacks in the corner. "What's all this?"

"We couldn't fit everything in the cellar." There were apples, carrots, potatoes, turnip, ginger, and garlic. Some they'd grown, others were used as trades for beef or other crops.

North pulled out a pocketknife from his back pocket, flicking it open. The blade gleamed in the moonlight. He grabbed an apple and carved off a slice to eat.

Colt dropped to his back, his arms behind his head as a makeshift pillow. His sweater rose up, exposing the lower half of his ripped abs and the dark trail of hair disappearing into his Wranglers.

Eva had hoped they'd take control once alone with her. Her body was a hormonal mess, her thoughts continually drifting to her basest desires. She didn't want to spell out the fact that she wanted them to fuck her. How could they have forgotten their night in the city?

"Why'd you bring us here, Eva?" asked Colton.

"So, we can be alone."

She couldn't walk away once the roast was over, not after seeing them all evening. All her old perceptions had changed, and they were no longer just North and Colt, her best friends from the next ranch over. They were her everything, not to mention the perfect specimens of the male form—tall, strong, and muscular. She thought back to all the times she'd seen them working under the sun in just their blue jeans or the many nights they'd slept cuddled beside her in nothing but fitted boxer briefs. How had she managed to look past those devastatingly good looks for so long?

"It's getting late. What do you want to do?" asked North.

"I want you both to make love to me."

"Here?"

"Here."

Colt shifted to his side, cupping her cheek in his big hand. "I want a lot more than this night, Eva."

"I know. I'm giving you all of me—tonight and forever."

North squatted down next to her. "People will talk. You don't even know if your own parents will approve."

"It's better than the alternative." Eva leaned close enough to steal a kiss from Colt. He didn't push her away as she half expected, but he kissed her back. She moaned into his mouth, loving the feel of his lips and brush of his tongue.

"God, I've missed you, baby girl." He kissed her with passion, the length of his body pressed against her. She closed her eyes, absorbing how good it felt to be in Colton's good graces again.

When he attempted to unbutton her jeans, she immediately helped him, not wanting him to change his mind. Her body was hotwired, her pussy contracting in distracting waves. North tugged her pants clean off her body, her bare legs breaking out into gooseflesh from the cool evening air.

She reached into the big pockets of her sweater coat and pulled out a small tube of lube, handing it to Colton.

"Where'd you get that?"

"You left it in the silver bullet."

North settled on her other side. He brushed her

hair to the side and peppered kisses along the back of her neck. "Tell us what you want, Eva." His voice was gruff, making her even needier. She could feel their feral desire all around her.

"I want both of you," she said. "Together."

"We're both here." Colt's hand drifted south, his fingers slipping under the waist of her panties. She parted her legs, hoping to guide him to where she needed him. Her inner folds were already swollen and moist, preparing for what was to come.

"That's not what I mean." Eva remembered how it felt when Colton had penetrated her asshole with a finger. It had created a wild burst of sensation that was incomparable. And she figured it was the only way for her to truly marry their ménage à trois. She wanted to feel both men claim her, binding them together in new, wondrous ways. Surely they'd been curious of the same thing. She'd heard other people talk about the pleasures of anal sex, so it couldn't be too bad—even if Colton and North were hung like horses.

"Tell me, sweet thing." Colt bent two fingers into her pussy. She grabbed his shoulder, digging her nails in as he pushed harder. Eva couldn't even answer, not with her inner walls pulsing around his invading fingers. She wanted to cry out for more but managed to keep a measure of composure.

"I want both of you to have sex with me."

"We can do that," said North with a growl. He tugged off her bulky sweater, trailing kisses along her bare shoulder blades. Shivers skittered along her skin as his rough hands roamed along her exposed curves. She felt surrounded, warm, and sexually alive.

"This time you're mine first." Colt rolled her clit between his fingers, making her gasp for air. He knew exactly how to touch her, as if he knew her body better than she knew herself. "I've been dreaming about you since Chester."

She shook her head, barely capable of speech. It felt so good to be wanted and desires. "No, I can take both of you at the same time."

"You can't handle both of us, Eva. It's best to take turns," said Colt.

"I really need both of you."

North pushed down her panties and smoothed his hand over the globe of her ass. "It'll hurt too much."

Just the feather light touch of North's finger along the seam of her ass made her see stars. "Don't stop," she murmured. Colton's fingers fucking her pussy, with the addition of North's forbidden touch, stole all her inhibitions. She wanted to experience everything, and she wouldn't take *no* for an answer.

North trailed some of the natural juices trickling down her inner thighs back to her ass. He caressed her nether hole until she gasped for air. "If we do this, you'll need to be prepared first." As he pressed his finger all the way into her rear, she clamped down on him, loving the feel of the foreign object in her asshole. "Shit, you're tight, baby."

"More," she said.

The men kissed her, crowded her, and continued to mimic the sex act with just their fingers.

"I'll whittle some of that ginger," said North.

"Good call," said Colton.

She had no clue what they were agreeing on, but North got up, tossed his shirt, and headed over to the burlap sacks in the corner. He went to work, carving one of the roots, rather than rejoining them.

"What's he doing?" she asked Colton. He rolled over her, positioning his body between her legs. Her panties slid back into place when she spread her legs, but it didn't stop her from rubbing her pussy against his denim-clad cock.

"He's fashioning a plug to prepare you. The oil from the ginger will dull the pain." He kissed all over her face, not solely from raw passion, but adoration. She could feel the mix of sexual love and the same unconditional McReed acceptance she'd known for a lifetime. It was beautiful and addicting.

North returned, his chest bare and jeans low on his hips. His body was hard and lean-muscled, no extra fat. "You can still change your mind, Eva. I won't care."

"I want to."

She knew the McReed brothers were unorthodox and had strong sexual appetites, if all the stories in town were true. But now they were hers, and hers alone, and she delighted in all their expertise.

"Roll her to her belly," said North.

Colton did as asked, rising to his knees so he could turn her over. She rested on her forearms until a strong hand to her back forced her to lie flat on her stomach. Her panties were slid down her thighs until off her body, leaving her completely nude on the old patchwork quilt. One or both of the twins rubbed her bottom, patting it enough to make it jiggle. The friction travelled all the way around to her clit.

"Get ready for his," said North. "It's gonna sting, but it'll make things easier for later."

Colt kissed her forehead, rubbing circles on her back as North pressed a dollop of lube against her asshole. "It's an old cowboy trick, baby girl."

"Do it," she squeaked, not wanting her nerves to take over.

The ginger root burned her delicate anal tissues as North slowly pressed it against her rear entrance. He moved in such tiny increments she questioned if he moved at all.

"Relax, Eva, or it'll feel worse. Bear down."

She did as asked, trusting both brothers completely. Eva pushed back against the invading phallus. Her breath picked up along with her rising nerves. She reminded herself that this was exactly what she wanted, and real cowgirls didn't wimp out from a little pain.

After a few minutes, the homemade plug slipped past her unforgiving sphincter muscle, lodging into place. She gasped, then sighed, knowing the hardest part was over. The entire time Colton cooed in her ear, giving her the strength she needed.

"Perfect fit," said North. "Now don't clench down on it or it'll burn. Just keep nice and limber."

"It gets better," Colton whispered in her ear. "Promise."

She trusted Colt's promises, and hoped he trusted hers. This was the beginning of something beautiful. Never in her life did she imagine getting hitched to the McReed twins. Now she realized they were her only possible future.

They rolled her to her back. The butt plug shifted inside her, a mix of pleasure and pain.

"Open your legs, Eva. I want to see your pretty little pussy." Colt helped spread her legs open at the knees. "Fucking gorgeous. Look at that, North."

Both men knelt before her open legs, her most intimate parts on display for them. She wasn't embarrassed like she knew she'd be with a boyfriend. Colton and North were so much more, a second protective skin.

"She's pink and swollen." North petted her pussy, his fingers gently caressing her engorged folds.

Eva felt dirty and wanton. She savored the twins'

attention, relieved they no longer pushed her away. Tonight, she'd make them hers.

Chapter Fifteen

North couldn't tear his eyes away from Eva's splayed legs. Her pussy was ripe and the bulbous end of the ginger root protruded from her asshole. It was erotic as hell.

She wriggled, getting accustomed to the foreign invasion. Her skin was pale in the moonlight, her stomach smooth and nipples beaded tight. She was a vision, and his cock had never been harder. He'd have to keep a tight rein on himself tonight. Eva was still inexperienced and he wanted to introduce her to new things slowly. But his patience was already being tested when he wanted nothing more than to sink into her tight little cunt.

"How does it feel now?" he asked.

"Not so bad." She reached her arms out for him. "Kiss me."

He lowered along the side of her, intertwining his fingers with hers. He kissed her on the mouth, losing himself in her sweet taste. North had never known what it felt like to really love a woman, and he never expected to. The entire idea of marriage and commitment turned him off after what he'd witnessed at home growing up. Although he'd had plenty of girlfriends and one-nighters over the years, the best of those experiences paled in comparison to one kiss from Eva Ford. He loved her so much it scared him.

When Eva opened her mouth, her fingers tightening around his, he knew Colt had gone down on her. He saw his brother's blond head buried between her legs. She kept her knees loose, her head tossed back, and eyes closed.

It was time to bring her to a higher level to

prepare her for their dual invasion. He was still unsure if a true ménage à trois was a good idea for such a tight, young thing. But Eva wanted it to happen and, of course, there was nothing North wanted more.

He collected both her thin wrists in one hand, bringing them above her head. He kept them locked in place as he descended on her exposed breasts. North suckled her tits, her mewling cries exciting him. She writhed and arched, the ginger root doing its job in preparing her.

"I like it," she chanted. "Oh God…"

"You like it when Colt eats your pussy?"

"Yes!"

"I can't wait to fuck you, baby girl."

She began to pant, an orgasm not far off. Colt pulled away before she could reach that peak. They needed her wound tight before attempting to double-fuck her.

"Why'd you stop?" she asked.

Colt hovered over her body. "You have to wait, little miss."

"I'm ready. I want you both. *Please.*"

"It'll be different with two men, Eva. There will be two cocks buried deep inside you." He kissed between her breasts. "You'll be filled to overflowing."

"Have you shared a woman before?" Eva asked.

North didn't expect her to ask about their sexual past. She knew they'd been around because they never hid it from her. But he'd never shared a woman with Colt. This was as new for them as it was for Eva.

"You're the first," Colt said. "And the last."

The threesome came about so naturally that North never stopped to consider the public reaction. Colton wanted to talk about the consequences when they were in Chester, but North had brushed him off. Sharing felt right, a logical progression for North, his twin, and Eva. He only hoped Mr. Ford didn't run them off. It would mean losing Eva *and* the family he'd grown to love.

"Take that thing out," said Eva. "I want the real thing."

North settled on the quilt beside Eva and kicked off his jeans. "Come straddle me," he said. He knew Colt would want to take her virgin hole this time around, and it was only fair.

She twisted to her hands and knees, crawling over his body, her long hair tickling his skin. "I love you," she said, kissing his stomach and chest as she travelled higher.

"Never leave me," he said before kissing her lips. It would destroy him to lose her now.

"Why would I?"

He held her close, loving the warm skin to skin contact. Mentioning his worries and fears about Mr. Ford's reaction to her news would only douse their rising passion.

North held the base of his cock, guiding Eva lower. "Sit on me, sweetheart. Go nice and slow."

"Take the ginger out."

"Colt'll take it out in a minute. Come on now." He was getting anxious, his balls pulling tight to his body. All he could think about now was Eva's pussy sinking down over his erection.

She was sopping wet, easily slipping into position. She eased her weight down, her tight walls hugging him in a welcome embrace. He groaned, holding her hips as she lowered all the way to the hilt. It felt like heaven.

"I love how that feels," she said. "You're so big. You take away my ache."

"Good girl," he said. "You're just perfect."

Eva rose up and came down slowly. It was exquisite torture. "Am I doing it right?"

"Yes, baby. Keep going."

His eyes lolled back in his head as she worked his erection. She was a beautiful sight, her perk breasts bouncing slightly each time she came down. He could see Colton standing behind her, carefully lubing up his cock. North was worried they'd hurt Eva, but he also trusted his brother to have her best interest in mind.

After a few minutes of teasingly slow sex, Colton joined them.

"Lean forward, Eva. I'm taking the ginger out now." His twin pressed her down so she was chest to chest with North, his cock bending inside of her.

North could feel the pressure ease when Colton plucked the plug out of her ass.

"Better?" he asked.

She was quiet at first, not answering. "I feel empty now. Empty and tingly, Colt."

"I'm going to put my cock inside your ass now. You sure you want to try this?"

"I have to get used to it now, because I plan to have a lot of it."

Her grip on North's shoulders tightened when Colton knelt behind her, getting himself in the right place.

****

Colton had allowed his twin to take Eva's virginity. Now he planned to take her ass for the first time, and he practically came just thinking about it. Her little asshole was open for him, thanks to the ginger plug. With his cock thoroughly lubed up, the introduction should be as painless as possible for Eva.

He pressed the broad head of his cock between her cheeks, only pushing in about an inch before giving her a break. She was tighter than fuck with North's big dick already waiting inside her. When Eva had first suggested they double-team her, his cock instantly sprang to life. It was a fantasy of every man. Add the fact he loved Eva more than he did himself, and he was raring to go.

"You okay?" he asked, after pushing in another long inch.

"Stop babying me, Colt. I'm hot all over, and you're killing me going so slow."

His twin lifted a brow, just as surprised by Eva's eagerness as him. He kept going until the full length of his cock was inside her, along with North. The fit was incredibly tight around him.

"How's that?" he asked.

Eva made a strangled sound, a mix of a gasp and a moan. "I'm so full. I think I'm going to come."

"Shit, not yet, darlin'," said North. "Let us have a bit of fun first."

They began to work her body. It was awkward at first getting used to the logistics, but once they'd decided on a position the developed a steady rhythm. They fucked her good, pistoning in and out of her pussy and ass like a well-oiled machine. It was true they'd never shared a woman in bed, but it all proceeded naturally, like they were meant to have Eva sandwiched between them. Colton felt like the luckiest man in the world.

The pressure in his balls grew to intolerable levels. Although his body was ready for release, he wanted to go on all night long. He was enjoying her too much to stop now.

"More," she cried. He could feel her ass spasming around him, warning of her imminent orgasm. Colton couldn't wait to feel her milk their cocks simultaneously. They moved faster, thrusting vigorously in Eva's willing body. All three of them were a mass of limbs and overheated flesh. It was perfect.

He nipped the back of her shoulder, reaching around to knead her breast. The further they got into the sex act, the rougher and more animalistic they all became. Little Eva could take a hard fucking and still demanded more.

"I love your ass. Do you like me fucking your ass, baby girl?"

"Yes," she gasped.

"You're all ours now. Every inch of you." He wanted to own her, love her, protect her, and keep her as theirs. Never had one human meant so much to him.

"It's happening!" she shouted as if afraid of the intensity of her impending release.

"Don't fight it," Colton said. "Relax and let your body guide you through it."

She came hard, her body suddenly bucking to a sharp halt, her ass clamping down on his dick without mercy. Then she exploded. Eva screamed with every contraction, the feminine sound turning him on like never before. As her inner walls kneaded both of them, Colton finally came, his hot cum spraying on and on into Eva's ass. The relief was instantaneous. He groaned as every last seed spilled inside her, along with every ounce of his energy.

Colton dropped to the side in a boneless mass, his body slick with sweat, and his heart racing.

They all lay there side by side, looking up at the stars through the cracks in the roof boards. It was quiet, peaceful, and like always, nothing needed to be said. He didn't have to promise Eva tomorrow, or remind her she was more than sex. She already knew.

The following Monday, Colton was back to work. North was next to him on horseback as they herded Mr.

Ford's tagged cattle into the holding pen. It was a bitch separating them from the younger stock, but they'd nearly gotten the job done. Since the ice was broken at the corn roast on Friday, and they had their plowing done at home, it was only right to help out the Fords as they always had. They couldn't let their fears and doubts control their lives.

"Truck is here," called Eva, standing on middle rung of the fence. "Dad said to let them through."

Colt lifted the second gate so the cattle could get into the second, smaller holding area. This herd was being shipped off, and it would mean less workload during the long winter months.

Once they'd got the last cow in the right place, Colton dismounted and walked his horse to the water trough. North came by a few minutes later.

"You still going to borrow Mr. Ford's excavator?"

"I thought you agreed it was a good idea."

Colton had been doing a lot of soul searching as of late. There were so many changes happening that his head was spinning. They'd talked with their mother on the phone Saturday and, for the first time in years, she sounded like a regular woman. She was happy living with her sister, enjoying her new beginning of sorts. Although she had a long road of counselling and therapy yet, she was on the mend. Colton expected she'd want to come home as soon as possible, but it cut him to hear she never wanted to return back to their town or the house of horrors, as she called it.

That's when he decided it was bullshit living in a home based on memories of pain and suffering. He wanted to tear the shitty little house to the ground and start new and fresh...hopefully with Eva. They still had a small guest cabin out back that was used as a home by earlier McReeds before the main house was built. It was only one room, but it would do until they could start rebuilding in the spring.

"Mr. Ford will think we've lost our fucking minds," said North.

"He knows more than you think. I don't think he'll question it."

They leaned against the fence, watching the cattle being herded up the ramp into the cattle car of the big rig by the buyers. The hooves echoed on the metal grating, drowning out all other sounds.

"Mom said to come in for lemonade." Eva leaned between them from behind.

"Hey, pretty girl." Colton turned to kiss her on the lips. She was always a ray of sunshine in his day. When North elbowed him in the ribs he noticed Mr. Ford watching as he stood in the distance talking with the driver of the truck. At first, he was afraid he'd been caught with his hand in the cookie jar. They'd always kissed Eva, but not intimately on the lips like Mr. Ford just witnessed.

He decided to play it off. What was the worst that could happen? He had to find out eventually, and Colton would have to deal with the aftermath regardless.

"Hurry, I have something good to tell both of you." Eva returned to the house, her pigtail swishing back and forth as she ran off. She was so fucking cute.

Colt could use a drink after rounding up cattle all morning. As they cut across the yard, a pick-up pulled in. Luke Weston hopped out, slammed the driver's side door, and walked towards them while adjusting his white Stetson. *The knight in fucking armor,* Colton thought.

"Mornin'," he said in greeting.

"Can we help you?" asked Colton, blocking his path.

He shrugged. "Looking for Eva. Where's she at?"

His hackles rose. Colton was no longer willing to play dead and let his insecurities rule his life. Eva was his, and nothing or no one would stand in their way. Luke may be the better man on paper, but no one would love Eva more than him and North.

"I don't know what happened last Friday, but Eva ain't looking for a man."

Luke frowned. "Her daddy says otherwise, so it's really none of your business, McReed." His demeanor changed, a challenge written on his face.

North shoved him unexpectedly. "Get in your damn truck and get off the fucking property. Got it?"

Colton stretched his arm out to the side to bar his brother from acting. Luke was right. Mr. Ford approved of him, even going so far as to set him up with Eva without her knowledge. Colton could barely sleep at night playing the scenarios over and over in his head. What would happen when Eva told her father she loved them? He couldn't stand to see disappointment in the eyes of the only man he considered a father figure.

"What the fuck is going on here? Are you her brothers now?"

"We're more to Eva than you'll ever be," said North.

Luke wasn't the sweet boy next door. He had the reputation as a stuck-up asshole who believed he deserved everything handed to him. In high school he'd always looked down on him and North like second class citizens because they didn't have the latest Dodge or name brand jeans.

"If I'm not mistaken, the two of you should be worried about your own house before meddling in others'. I think the only thing the two of you are capable of is running people off."

"You referring to our mama?" asked Colton, lowering his arm and stepping forward.

"Who's next? Is Eva your next victim? I don't know why Mr. Ford allows you underfoot around here at all. You're a couple of worthless drunks."

He was a fraction of a second away from throwing the first punch. Every cell in his body craved to fight, to expel all his bottled-up pain on Luke Weston. But he was a fraction of a second too slow.

"Take it easy," called Mr. Ford. The rumble of the big rig's engine quieted as it distanced down the back road. Eva's father cut across the yard towards them, the little Shih Tzu rushing to keep up behind him. "There won't be any fighting going on here today, boys."

"Good morning, sir. I just came to call on Eva, but for some reason, the McReed brothers want me to leave."

Mr. Ford nodded thoughtfully, looking them each up and down. He rubbed the scruff on his chin as if debating his next move. He was always calm, slow to anger, and fair. "Sometimes I jump the gun when it comes to my little girl. Eva ain't too eager for me to interfere in her love life. She gave me a tongue lashing about it just this morning. You understand, son?"

"Are you sure about that?" asked Luke. "We seemed to get along just fine."

"You heard the man!" snapped North.

Mr. Ford held up a hand to silence North. "I'm very sure. She doesn't want me choosing her men any more than she wants me telling her how to live her life. And I tend to agree."

Luke tipped his hand and sulked back to his truck. Colton knew he wanted to argue and fight, but he couldn't do so in front of Mr. Ford. He was a respected cattle rancher, just as his father was known in the pork industry.

After the pick-up disappeared in a billow of dust down the road, Eva's father turned to face both of them. He took a deep breath before speaking. "How many times have I told you two about controlling your tempers? You gain nothing from fighting and making enemies."

"Yes, sir," they answered in unison.

Mr. Ford checked his watch before loosening his collar. "Just about time for lunch. You wanted to ask me something earlier, Colton?"

He had to think for a minute to remember what he referred to. "I wanted to borrow the big excavator this week. I'd have it back by Friday at the latest."

"Big project?"

Colton said nothing at first, embarrassed of the truth. "We're doing a little remodelling," he said. "It's time to say goodbye to the old house."

He placed a hand on Colton and North's shoulders, giving a little squeeze. He looked almost teary-eyed, or was it the sun in his eyes? "You boys have been through hell and back, I won't deny that. But you've come a long way, and I'm proud of you. No less proud than a father of his flesh and blood sons."

Colton's throat clogged with emotion. Mr. Ford's acceptance and love were more important to him than he originally imagined. He'd been there for them when nobody else was. "Sir..."

"Take the excavator and tear the bastard to the ground if that's what you need to do. But don't forget that there's always something better on the horizon. You're both young with the whole world ahead of you."

He wanted to tell Mr. Ford that the only light he needed in his life was in the form of his daughter. Life without her would be void of color. Instead he kept his mouth shut.

"Now, let's go have some lunch," he said. The three of them walked side by side towards the white brick house. It was the one place all his good memories were made. A place he wanted to preserve for all time to come.

"I'm sorry about the thing with Luke Weston," said Colton. "Sometimes it's hard to control myself where Eva is concerned."

"I suppose that was my fault, so I'll take the blame. But Eva has a strong mind of her own and can most certainly speak for herself."

"That's true," said North. "She doesn't hold back."

They reached the house and Mr. Ford opened the whiny screen door. He stopped before entering, taking a cleansing breath. Without turning around, he spoke, "I trust my daughter's judgement. I respect her choices. And you boys have never let me down."

It was all he had to say for Colton to know Eva had spilled the news. The black cloud hovering over his life had finally broken.

Epilogue

Eva sat cross-legged in the tall grass, the gentle breeze carrying notes of pine and black earth. North's head rested on her lap, and she enjoyed running her fingers through his thick hair.

Colton leapt down from the excavator and walked towards them, using his Stetson to swat away the dust on his jeans. "All done. I'll start the cleanup next week."

The McReed house was a massive pile of lumber and rubble in the large clearing. Eva didn't question their decision to destroy the old bungalow. She'd only had a few glimpses of their harsh home life, and it was enough to understand why they wanted to erase the past.

"Do you feel any different?" asked Eva.

He dropped down onto his side next to her. "Darlin', I'm not sure I have any feelings left."

"Of course you do, silly."

Colton looked up at her, tapping the tip of her nose. "Just enough for you."

Eva smiled. Her world was at peace. She'd proved to her father that she was a woman, capable of making her own choices. And she was free to love the two cowboys who held her heart.

"We'll be busy come spring," said North, shifting to his back. He looked up at her with those dark, narrow eyes. She trailed her fingertip along the scruff on his jaw, tracing all his masculine features. Just looking at the gorgeous cowboy did wild things to her libido. His every detail was an aphrodisiac, from the hard bulge in his Wranglers to the uncommon broadness of his shoulders in his padded jacket. She couldn't stop herself from imagining him supporting his weight over her prone body, every muscle flexing and tense.

"Where should we start building?" asked Colt, pulling her from her reverie.

"Maybe to the east, closer to the river," said North.

"I like it over there," said Eva. "We used to fish for smelts every year. Remember?"

"And you refused to eat them."

"They were too cute to eat."

North hoisted himself up enough to steal a kiss. She closed her eyes and savored the moment. She could smell his rich cologne when he moved, and his lips tasted of spearmint.

Colt tugged her until she fell to her back, the soft grass cushioning her fall. "I guess the bunker will be home for at least six months." He smoothed the hair from her face, staring at her intently. The sunlight reflected off the ocean in his eyes, mesmerizing her. He'd been through so much, they both had, and she hoped their pain was less now that they were all moving on.

"I have a feeling mom and dad will insist we stay at my place. You know, with the toilet and running water and all."

Colt shrugged, hovering over the left side of her body. "As long as I have you, I'm good. And I don't have to return you *or* the excavator until dinner hour. Until then, you're ours."

He began to tickle her sides, not letting her escape. She kicked her legs and attempted to fend the twins off, but failed, only able to scream and laugh out loud.

"That's the sound," said North when they finally let her breathe.

"What sound?"

"Your laughter is the most beautiful thing in the world." North kissed the side of her neck, his tongue teasing the shell of her ear.

"That feels good," she whispered. Would she always feel this way? Would her body always light up from just the sound of their deep voices?

"Baby girl, I can show you things you never knew existed."

Eva was putty in the capable hands of the McReed brothers. She eagerly awaited their lessons, the slow and precise introduction into their world of sexual pleasure.

Colton brought her hand to his denim-covered crotch. He was harder than oak, and knowing she was the reason for it excited her. "Feel that? That's what you do to me."

She turned her head and licked the seam of his lips, giving him a little nip. "Good. Then you won't be pushing me away anymore."

"Hell no. We're both yours, Eva Ford. It took me a lifetime to see what was right in front of me, and it'll take the rest of my life to show you how much you mean to me."

The McReed brothers enveloped her body with their strong arms, showering her with the affection she knew so well. Only now it heated her blood and stirred her soul. Eva had been searching for something when she'd had it all along—the perfect love.

The End

www.staceyespino.com

EVERNIGHT PUBLISHING ®

www.evernightpublishing.com

www.ingramcontent.com/pod-product-compliance
Lightning Source LLC
Chambersburg PA
CBHW032205190626
46810CB00018B/1568